A Candlelight Ecstasy Romance®

"CAROL—HEY! WHAT ARE YOU DOING?" HARLAN YELLED AS THE PAPERWEIGHT JUST MISSED HIS HEAD.

"Oh! You scared me half to death!" she cried, leaning on her desk.

"How do you think I feel?" he replied as he picked up her makeshift weapon and replaced it on the desk.

"I don't care how you feel. I just want to know how you got in here."

"I sweet-talked a security guard," Harlan admitted cheerfully. "I've come to kidnap you. Sunday is a day of rest, and we're going to have some of that fun you've missed out on."

"Harlan, I can't," she protested. "I've got too much work—"

He silenced her with a firm kiss. "Don't be ridiculous. Even stockbrokers need some fun in their lives, and you're going to have it. Now, do I kidnap you or do I make love to you on your office carpet?"

She couldn't miss the gleam in his eyes. "You'd do it, wouldn't you?"

"In a flash."

CANDLELIGHT ECSTASY ROMANCES®

LOVE MAKES THE DIFFERENCE

Emily Elliott

A Candlelight Ecstasy Romance®

Published by
Dell Publishing Co., Inc.
1 Dag Hammarskjold Plaza
New York, New York 10017

ISBN: 0-440-13774-8

Printed in the United States of America

May 1986

10 9 8 7 6 5 4 3 2 1

WFH

To Our Readers:

We have been delighted with your enthusiastic response to Candlelight Ecstasy Romances®, and we thank you for the interest you have shown in this exciting series.

In the upcoming months we will continue to present the distinctive sensuous love stories you have come to expect only from Ecstasy. We look forward to bringing you many more books from your favorite authors and also the very finest work from new authors of contemporary romantic fiction.

As always, we are striving to present the unique, absorbing love stories that you enjoy most—books that are more than ordinary romance. Your suggestions and comments are always welcome. Please write to us at the address below.

Sincerely,

The Editors
Candlelight Romances
1 Dag Hammarskjold Plaza
New York, New York 10017

LOVE MAKES THE DIFFERENCE

CHAPTER ONE

Carol Venson stared at the numbers on her computer terminal and frowned as she stubbed out her cigarette. Tedelco Common had fallen again—it had just come through on her terminal and been announced on the squawk box simultaneously. Three of her major clients had considerable investments in that particular stock, and she had to let them know immediately. Sighing, she lowered the volume on the speaker that transmitted the ups and downs from the floor of the stock exchange in New York and unclipped the large gold earring on her left ear. She picked up the telephone receiver with one hand while she rifled through her Rolodex with the other. Finding what she wanted, she punched in a number with her manicured nail and drummed her fingers on her desk while Howard Jenkins's secretary paged him. "Hello, Howard, this is Carol Venson. How are you?"

"Fine, until you called," Howard teased. Carol smiled as she pictured the friendly, middle-aged Mercedes dealer. "What's up?"

"Tedelco Common is falling," Carol said. "Do you want to hang on or sell?"

"Sell," Howard said immediately. "I want to put it into something that's holding steady or going up a little."

Carol nodded and made a note to herself. "Does it matter what I put it into?"

"Come up with three or four possibilities, why don't you?" Howard suggested. "Call me before you buy anything."

"Sure thing, Howard," she replied. "I'll get back to you later today." They wished each other a good morning and Carol looked up another number on her Rolodex. Grimacing a little, she placed another call and was greeted with Laura Parker's whiny drawl.

"Hello, Laura, this is Carol Venson," she said. "How are you today?"

"Oh, fine, just fine, dear. Are you calling about one of Theodore's investments?" Though Theodore Parker had been dead for nearly three years, Laura still persisted in referring to her considerable wealth as though it were his.

"I'm afraid so, Laura," Carol said. "Tedelco Common is falling. Do you want me to sell?"

There was momentary silence on the other end of the line, and Carol could picture Laura biting her lip. "Oh, my, Carol, what do you think I should do? Theodore always said that you shouldn't be too hasty, but I would hate to lose money. Theodore worked so hard to earn it, you know."

"Yes, I do know, and that's why we're trying to manage it properly," Carol said. "If it were me, I'd sell."

It took Laura fifteen minutes of hemming and hawing, but in the end she decided to go along with Carol and sell. Carol expelled the breath she had been holding as she dialed the third number. Laura was a dear, but she had so much trouble making up her mind, and that kind of indecision drove Carol up the wall. She much preferred working with businesspeople who knew how to make a decision.

Carol spoke briefly to Wendell Robbin's secretary, and glanced through the *Wall Street Journal* for a second time, listening to the squawk box with one ear, while she waited for Wendell to finish with his patient. When he did come on the line, Carol explained the situation to him, and after a brief discussion he decided to keep the stock for a few more days and see what it would do. Carol accepted his decision without argument and wished him a good day. She hadn't really expected Wendell to sell. He was one of her more conservative clients, slow to buy and even slower to sell. Sometimes she wished he were a little more daring with his investments, but his philosophy had earned him a steady income and Carol a reliable commission.

Carol wrote off two tickets to the wire operator, who would enter them into another computer that was connected to the exchange floor in New York. By the end of the afternoon, probably sooner, the stock would be sold and checks on the way to Howard and Laura. Carol clipped her earring back on and went to the office where the wire operator transmitted the sales.

"I have a couple of tickets for you," she said as she handed them to Bennie Johnson, her favorite operator.

"Will do," Bennie said. His ebony face lit up with a wide smile. "What's your Kimberly been up to this week?" he asked as his eyes danced mischievously.

Carol returned Bennie's grin. Her daughter and Bennie's son were the same age and had just graduated from rival high schools, and she and Bennie were engaged in a little friendly rivalry of their own as they frequently reported the ups and downs of their children. Kimberly Venson, who was starting the University of Houston in the fall, was the apple of her mother's eye, even if she was just an average student. Carol suspected that Kimberly had it in her to do better academically than she had in the past, and hoped that the additional challenge of college might spur her on. Ronnie Johnson was a downright poor student but was such a fine football player several colleges were willing to take him in spite of his poor grades.

Carol looked at Bennie expectantly. "Come on, Bennie. You're just dying to brag about something."

"Ronnie's decided on Texas A&M," Bennie said shyly.

"Hey, that's super!" Carol enthused. "Good thing he doesn't take after his skinny old dad, isn't it?"

"Yeah, he got all that from Clara's side of the family," Bennie admitted. "That girl of yours, though, she's just like you."

"Thanks, Bennie," Carol said softly. "I've tried hard to raise her well."

"And it hasn't always been easy being a single parent, has it?" Bennie asked.

Carol rolled her eyes. "Well, it was easier without her father around," she said dryly. "I've got to get back to work. See you later."

Carol stopped by the water fountain and took her ulcer medication. Then she returned to her office for lunch. Since she and her fellow stockbrokers seldom left their offices for long periods during trading hours, she ate a sandwich and a banana at her desk between calls to her numerous clients, always keeping part of her attention on the squawk box and the terminal. After the last call, she took a few minutes to glance around her plush office, one of the perks her company had given her after almost eight years as one of their most successful stockbrokers.

Carol was proud of herself for having earned this office. She was pleased with this job, in fact, even if the job itself frequently was not much to her liking. She had gotten a late start, but finally, at the age of thirty-seven, she had accomplished what she had set out to do—she had made something out of Carol Venson and she would be able to give Kimberly the start in life that she deserved. Although Kim wasn't the student Carol had been, she was a girl that any mother could be proud of, and Carol intended to see to it that Kim had every chance for a wonderful future.

But Carol did have one worry. Kim had met a young man last fall and had been dating him steadily ever since. Brandon Stone was an extremely good-looking boy, and certainly nice enough to both Carol and Kim, but he had been out of high school for over a year and still had not started college. From what Kim had said, Brandon worked for his father as a tree trimmer, and Kim had been vague every time Carol had tried to question her about the young man's plans for the future. Carol had been tempted several times to insist that Kim date other boys from her school, but since she really had no concrete objections to Brandon, other than his lack of future plans, she had held her tongue and greeted Brandon with the same friendly courtesy she showed all of Carol's friends, keeping her doubts about him to herself and hoping that Kim would outgrow the boy in time.

Turning back to her work, Carol got out a list of prospective clients she had been meaning to call. She heard an announcement of a falling stock on the squawk box and was making a note to call another client about the changing price when her boss rapped lightly on the door.

"Come in," Carol said.

Harold Rhodes entered and sat down in the chair across from Carol, crossing one leg over the other. Carol sighed inwardly, careful not to let her expression show her chagrin as she smiled expectantly at her resident thorn in the flesh. Harold Rhodes was one of the reasons her job as a stockbroker was not the most pleasant in the world. A perfectionist by nature, he believed that high, almost unrealistic goals should be set and reached every year by each of his brokers, and he would come by regularly and "discuss" these with his employees, pushing them to achieve even more than they had been. Carol, who felt that her six-figure income indicated she had plenty of motivation without being pushed by Harold, deeply resented these little discussions, and would invariably come away from them with a headache, a stomachache, or both.

"Hello, Harold," Carol said. "What can I do for you?"

Harold smiled what he thought was his genial smile. "Just thought I'd see how you were doing," he said. "We're halfway through the year, you know."

"I'm doing just fine, Harold," Carol said. "I've more than met my commission goals. My clients and I have had a very good year so far."

Harold leaned his elbows on the arm of the chair and bent his fingers into a steeple as he thought a minute. "Is it possible that your goals weren't high enough?" he asked. "Perhaps we ought to think about revising them upward."

Carol gritted her teeth and bit back a sharp retort. "If you'd care to check, you'll find that mine were as high as any of the other brokers with my years of experience," she said evenly. "I feel I've achieved quite a bit." Dear God, he couldn't ask her to revise hers upward! She was busting her rear to meet the goals she already had!

Harold cleared his throat. "I'm sure that's true," he said, resenting her polite but firm refusal. He looked over at the cool, composed woman who stared evenly at him and felt an unwilling admiration for her, both as a woman and as a stockbroker. Although he was a happily married man, he couldn't help but appreciate her feminine beauty. And she was right—she had outperformed almost all of the other brokers in the office. Still, if she was capable of bringing in that much more business, he wanted to see that she did. "So how about new clients? Have you signed up the number that we discussed in January?"

"Not quite," Carol admitted as she fought to keep irritation from showing on her face. She was constantly seeking new clients—they all were. With a twenty-percent attrition rate every year, a stockbroker had to sign new customers constantly if he or she wanted to hold steady. But she felt that Harold's previous suggestion of a fifty-percent increase by the end of the year was unrealistic.

Harold stayed for another thirty minutes, coming up with ways that Carol could add even more people to her already considerable list. By the time he finally left, Carol's head hurt and her stomach was churning. She fumbled around in her desk for a bottle of buffered aspirin and blessed her stomach pills for whatever good they were doing. Carol wondered if the pressure from Harold would ever let up. But she had a good job, she reminded herself. She was a successful stockbroker, and the constant tension was simply the price she had to pay for that. Besides, most of the time she drove herself harder than Harold ever thought of doing.

Carol kept one eye on the computer console on her desk as she flipped open her file of prospects. When she had first started with the company, she had spent most of the day on the telephone soliciting clients. She admitted to herself that she had neglected this part of her job for the last month or so, but her list already kept her very busy. Besides, she really didn't care for telephoning, since nine calls out of ten ended up with a total rejection. As she gritted her teeth and dialed again, she reminded herself that new clinets did sign with her and that about one call out of ten eventually landed her someone new. She just had to remember that it was all in the numbers.

Carol listened to the squawk box as she made her calls, breathing a sigh of relief when the exchange in New York closed at three Houston time and she could devote herself entirely to the calls. Damn Harold. If he thought she should sign more clients, then sign them she would. She was dialing her twentieth number when Travis, the assistant she shared with another broker, stuck his head in the door.

"Carol, I hate to bother you, but there's a man out here waiting to see you. He says he has to talk to you right now. It's urgent."

"Is he a client?" Carol asked as the telephone started to ring on the other end of the line.

Travis glanced back at the man. "Uh, no, I don't think so," he said.

But Travis didn't know that for sure. "Show him in," Carol said. "Hello, Mr. Hernandez? I'm Carol Venson, with the Purcell-Smith Brokerage Agency. Your name was given to me by Rusty Guajardo, and I wondered if we might talk a few minutes about using Purcell-Smith as your brokerage house." Out of the corner of her eye she saw a tall, dark-haired man come through the door. She stared in amazement at the blue-jeaned figure with a scowl on his face, and a shiver of foreboding crept down her spine. Whoever this man was, she was fairly sure he wasn't there to invest his money in the stock market.

Mr. Hernandez sounded interested, so Carol excused herself for a moment. "I'll be right with you," she said as she gestured the man to the chair in front of her desk.

"Mrs. Venson—"

"I'll be right with you," Carol repeated, ignoring the anger on the man's face when she turned away from him and spoke to Mr. Hernandez. Sensing that she had better not make the man wait too long, she briefly outlined the extent of her services, conscious of a pair of stormy blue eyes staring at her from under a shock of unruly black hair that was faintly tinged with gray.

Harlan Stone tried to control his anger and his impatience as he waited for Carol Venson to finish her phone call. He stared at her finely chisled profile, noting in spite of his state of mind that her cheekbones were high and her nose was short and straight like Kim's were, and her hair was the same rich shade of mahogany as Kim's, although it was cut into a short, fashionable style and did not hang long and free like her daughter's. Harlan couldn't help but appreciate the hint of feminine allure under the tailored business suit she wore, even though she was a little too thin for his taste. Yes, this woman had to be Kim Venson's mother, the resemblance was too striking to be coincidence. It had taken him awhile to remember that Brandon had said Kim's mother worked at a brokerage house, but once he remembered he had spent over two hours on the telephone calling every firm in Houston trying to track her down. Finally the operator at this office said that they did have a Carol Venson in their employ, and even then he wasn't sure it was the right Carol Venson. He stared for a moment at the woman, noting that her large brown eyes were reserved, yet at the same time she seemed pleased by the way her conversation was going. He hoped she enjoyed her few minutes of pleasure; she wasn't going to be happy with what he had to say to her.

Carol glanced at the man in her office as she picked up her appointment book. He still looked as angry as he had when he had marched in a few minutes ago, and she was sure that having to wait for her wasn't sweetening his temper. As she made an appointment for Mr. Hernandez to come to her office, she wondered—not for the first time—what the man was so angry about. Well, no doubt she'd know soon enough. She wished Mr. Hernandez a good day and turned to her visitor.

"I'm Carol Venson," she said as she stood up and extended her hand. "I'm sorry to keep you waiting. How may I help you today?"

The man stood and took Carol's hand, shaking it briefly. "I'm Harlan Stone," he said. Carol noticed the feel of rough callouses across his palm as he took her slender, manicured hand in his large, rough one. "Brandon's father. You *are* Kim's mother, aren't you?"

Harlan released her hand as Carol nodded, not particularly liking the way Harlan spit out her daughter's name. "Yes, I'm Kim's mother," she said, trying to ignore Harlan's hostility.

"Sit down, Mrs. Venson," he said. "I have a lovely little piece of news for you, and unless you already know about it, you might prefer to be sitting."

"What is it?" Carol demanded. "The kids—were they in an accident? Are they all right?"

"No, they weren't hurt or anything," Harlan said as he sat back down and motioned for Carol to do the same.

She sat down.

"I came home for lunch early this afternoon and overheard Kim and Brand making plans to elope tomorrow," Harlan said bluntly.

"What?" Carol yelled as she rose out of the chair. "Why would Kim be planning to do a thing like that? What could she possibly mean by running away with that boy?"

"Sit down, Mrs. Venson," Harlan said sharply. "I'm just as upset as you are, and yelling about it isn't going to do any good."

"I wasn't yelling," Carol said coldly as she sat back down. "Of course I'm upset. What on earth could those two be thinking of? Kim has a marvelous future ahead of her! She doesn't have any business getting married right now."

"I gathered from their conversation that neither one of them was looking forward to facing us with the rest of the good news," Harlan said as he reached up and rubbed his hand across his forehead. "Kim's pregnant."

Pregnant. Her Kim was pregnant? Carol's face paled to the point that even Harlan noticed. Oh, no, how could she have let that happen to her? "Are—are you sure?" she asked through stiff lips.

"Yes," Harlan said as he stood and paced around her office. "I overheard Brandon offer to go with Kim to tell you about the baby, but Kim said no and started to cry. Anyway, they're planning to leave together in the morning and drive to Mexico." He paused and faced her. "I want that marriage stopped."

Carol flinched at the scorn and contempt in his voice as he continued. "I don't expect you to let Brandon off easily, of course. He's in part responsible for the pregnancy and he'll help her financially and acknowledge the baby. But I won't have him trapped into a marriage by a scheming little brat who would do anything to get a boy like Brandon tied to her, just because he's handsome and already has a good job and a steady income. He can do without a little golddigger like that. Now, can I count on you to see that they don't leave together in the morning?"

Carol stood up and faced Harlan squarely, making no effort to hide her anger. "You can bet your last dollar I will, Mr. Stone. That uneducated hulk you call a son isn't good enough for my daughter to marry. Scheming little golddigger? Have you bothered to take a look at the clothes she wears or the sports car she drives? She can buy and sell that brat of yours in his beat-up pickup truck several times over, even without the investments I've made in her name. You're damn right, Mr. Stone. Kim's starting college this fall and has a marvelous future ahead of her. I'll lock her in her room before I let her tie herself to a loser like your kid."

"My kid's not a loser!" Harlan exclaimed defensively as he tried to hide his astonishment at Carol's tirade. His cheeks turned a dull shade of red as he glanced around her luxurious office and took another look at her expensive suit.

"And my kid's not a golddigger," Carol said softly. "She has no need to trap your son into marriage for his income or any other reason."

"I—I still don't think they should get married," Harlan stammered. "They're too young, they're—"

"You can spare me the arguments, Mr. Stone," Carol said. "I agree completely with you that the marriage shouldn't take place. Thank you for bringing this situation to my attention. I'll take care of it."

"We'll be over this evening at seven to talk about what needs to be done," Harlan said stiffly.

"There will be no need for that," Carol replied. "I said I would take care of it, and I will."

"But we need to talk about what's going to happen to Kim and the baby," Harlan persisted. "Brandon and I should be in on that decision."

"Don't you think Brandon has done enough already?" Carol snapped. "I *said* I would take care of this. Kim and I will decide what to do about the pregnancy. You and Brandon don't need to bother yourselves any further."

"Don't you think you're being a little presumptuous, Mrs. Venson?" Harlan asked coldly. "After all, that's my grandchild too."

"You weren't so eager to be a part of all this when you thought Kim was a little golddigger," Carol retorted. "And I don't think I'm being presumptuous, Mr. Stone. After all, I'll be the one footing the bill, not you or your son."

"I never said I didn't want him to be part of the solution, just that I didn't think the kids ought to get married," Harlan said. "We'll talk about that tonight." He shoved his hands in his pockets. "Mrs. Venson, I apologize for the crack about Kim being a golddigger. You're obviously offended and I was out of line. My only excuse is that I'm upset about this."

"You think I'm not?" Carol demanded, her eyes shimmering with tears. "Go home, Mr. Stone," she said tiredly. "And don't worry about my daughter. I'll take care of her."

"We'll see you at seven," Harlan said.

When he left, she collapsed into her chair, burying her face in her hands. Pregnant. Kim, her Kim, had made the same mistake Carol had made all those years ago. She had so passionately, so desperately wanted better for her daughter than that! And by Brandon Stone, of all people. He was probably a bigger loser than Jack Venson had been. Why? Why had Kim let it happen to *her?*

Carol fought back the tears that threatened to flood her eyes. She searched her memory as she thought about Kim's behavior for the last few weeks. Yes, the signs had been there that something was wrong—the moodiness, the quietness, the uneasiness that Carol could remember all too well as being the outward signs of the overwhelming terror that the unthinkable had happened. And she had been too absorbed with her job to even realize that something was seriously wrong. Sniffing, Carol composed herself and left her office for the day, though she usually stayed later, making calls and going through her mail. Harold Rhodes stared at her pointedly as she left and was rewarded with a scowl that had even him backing off a little.

Carol found her almond-color Lincoln in the parking garage, and with unseeing eyes battled the traffic that clogged the streets of downtown Houston. Pregnant. Exactly the same thing that had happened to Carol so many years ago. Carol flinched when a loud horn sounded behind her and inched through the intersection. Kim had made exactly the same mistake she had made.

Carol finally got on the expressway that would take her to her home in a Houston suburb. She usually hated fighting the traffic and looked forward to getting back to her beautiful home, but today she ignored the traffic, dreading the thought of having to confront Kim. She could understand Kim's reluctance to face her with the news—she hated talking to Kim about it almost as much as she was sure Kim dreaded having to tell her about the baby.

Carol left her car in the driveway and ran toward the house, fumbling a minute with her keys before she got the door unlocked. The cool air of the house met the hot skin of her face as she opened the front door and stepped inside. Her heels clicked on the tile floor as she made her way down the hall to Kim's bedroom.

"Kim? Are you home?"

"In here, Mom," Kim called through her closed bedroom door, her voice muffled.

Carol normally asked Kim's permission to enter, but today she threw open the door without warning. Kim had her over-night bag on the bed and was folding a pair of blue jeans.

"Uh, hi, Mom," she stammered. "Chrissi asked me if I'd like to spend tomorrow night at her place," she said. "I thought I'd go ahead and pack."

"Has Chrissi agreed to cover for you and Brandon?" Carol asked quietly. Kim's eyes grew wide. "Mr. Stone overheard you and Brandon in the kitchen today," she explained dully. "He said that you and Brandon were planning to elope because you were pregnant. Kim, is it true?"

Kim took one look at her mother's pinched, hurt face and the tears that she had been trying to stifle for the last two weeks overflowed in her eyes. "Oh, Mom, I'm sorry." She sobbed as she crumpled onto the bed. "I'm so sorry. I never meant to get pregnant. I never meant to hurt you like that."

CHAPTER TWO

Carol's eyes brimmed with tears as she sat down on the side of the bed and took her sobbing daughter into her arms. "Oh, Kim, don't worry about me," she soothed as she fought down her own deep hurt. "I'll be all right, mothers always are."

Kim turned and sobbed into Carol's shoulder. "Oh, Mom," she cried brokenly. "I've messed everything up and I'm sorry. You always had such hopes for me, and I've ruined it all."

"Hush now, don't you think like that," Carol murmured as she rocked Kim back and forth. "Your future's not a disaster, even though you must be feeling like that now."

"Brandon and I were going to wait until I got out of college before we got married," Kim said, her voice muffled into Carol's jacket. "Now we have to get married right away." She pulled back and sniffed. "We were going to Mexico tomorrow."

"Kim, you know that running away never solves anything," Carol reminded her. "You should have come to me the minute you suspected, or at least the minute you knew. When are you due?"

"In late November. Mom, I didn't come to you because I couldn't face you," Kim said. "I thought you would be so hurt."

"Kim, I'm all right," Carol said. "I hurt for you—that's different. Now, come get a glass of milk and let's talk about your options."

Kim followed her to the kitchen and Carol poured her a glass of milk. Carol would have loved a stiff shot of Scotch, but in deference to her stomach she poured herself a glass of cold water and sat across from Kim at the kitchen table.

"Feel better?" she asked when Kim had drained the glass.

Kim nodded.

"What happened, Kim?" Carol asked quietly. "You know I'm the last mother in the world who would condemn you for conceiving a baby out of wedlock, but why didn't you do something to prevent it? I've always told you that you could come to me or go to Dr. Scott when you felt you needed protection."

Kim shrugged. "You didn't like Brandon, and I knew you would know it was him. I was embarrassed."

"I never said I didn't like Brandon," Carol said.

"You didn't have to. The way you looked at his truck said it all."

"Were you too embarrassed to go to Dr. Scott?" Carol asked.

Kim nodded. "I felt guilty enough for doing it without having to face him or you."

"All right. It's water under the bridge anyway. We need to go forward from here and talk about your future," Carol said.

"I guess Brandon and I won't be eloping tomorrow," Kim said slowly. "We can get married here in Houston."

"That's what I wanted to talk to you about," Carol began as she sipped her water. "Kim, there's really no reason why you have to marry Brandon at all."

"But we're expecting a baby," Kim protested. "Besides, we love each other. We want to be together!"

Carol eyed her daughter sharply. Maybe Harlan Stone had been right. "Is that why you got pregnant? Were you trying to trap that boy into marriage?"

"Oh, Mother, no," Kim said. "But as long as I am pregnant, we may as well get married. We would have eventually, anyway."

"Kim, I know you think a lot of Brandon, but a hasty marriage at this point would be the worst thing you and that young man could do to yourselves. You have a wonderful future ahead of you, and there isn't any reason you should ruin that. Nowadays a pregnancy isn't the end of the world, you know."

"No!" Kim cried, clutching her stomach. "I couldn't have an abortion, I just couldn't!"

"Kimberly, I didn't mean that!" Carol cried. "There are other alternatives."

"I'm sorry," Kim said quietly. "I thought you might think of it as an easy way out."

"It would be, but you aren't made like that and neither am I," Carol said. "Have you thought of giving the baby up for adoption?"

"No way," Kim said stubbornly.

"Then the sensible thing for you to do is to go ahead and have it. You and I will raise it until you get married and leave home."

"No, Mother," Kim said firmly. "Brandon and I want to get married."

"Why?" Carol demanded. "I've already told you that you don't have to give up the baby. I'll help you raise your child. Just don't tie yourself to that boy for who knows how many wasted years!"

"They wouldn't be wasted with Brandon," Kim said stubbornly. "If you liked him you wouldn't mind."

"Kim, whether I do or don't like the boy is beside the point. Brandon is a good-looking young man and seems nice enough, but what kind of future does he have? Has he taken any steps to get an education? Does he have any ambition whatsoever?"

Kim's jaw thrust forward just a little. "He trims trees with his father. He's going to own the company someday."

"There's no future in a job like that," Carol said firmly. "You deserve better!"

"There's nothing wrong with what Brandon does," she said stubbornly. "I don't care what he does for a living. I love him."

"Kim, there is more to life than true love," Carol argued. "You don't want to spend your life with a man like him."

"Yes, I do," Kim insisted angrily.

"You think that now because you're pregnant," Carol said, deciding to try a new argument. "I felt that way about your father too, when I found out I was expecting you. But I was wrong, and I was trapped for ten years in a marriage with a man who was totally unsuitable for me. Please, Kim, don't rush into a marriage just because of the baby you're carrying."

"But Brandon and I love each other," Kim argued quietly. "Our minds are made up. We're going to get married, with or without your approval."

Carol was quiet for a minute as she chose her words carefully. "You know that I love you, Kimberly. And it's because I love you that I'm going to have to forbid you to marry Brandon Stone. He's just not the kind of young man that you have any business marrying. Mr. Stone feels the same way I do about the marriage."

"I'm going to marry Brandon," Kim said angrily, "with you or without you!"

"You do and I'll have it annulled," Carol said quietly. "And I'll have you on a plane to your aunt in California so fast it will make your head swim. I'm sorry, Kim. I'm going to have to say no."

Kim's eyes filled with tears and she dashed them away impatiently. "Damn you, Mother! For a few minutes there I thought you would understand!" She stormed out of the kitchen, tears running down her face.

Carol reached in her purse and withdrew a cigarette, lighting it and puffing nervously as she went to her bedroom. She sat down for a minute in her wicker chair, looking around at the tranquil room filled with a mixture of golden oak antiques and delicate wicker, and tried to absorb some of the peace she usually found there. She had hated talking to Kim that way. It was the first time in years that the two of them had been so at odds with one another, and Carol detested having to forbid the girl to marry. But she was doing it for Kim's own good, and Kim would realize it sooner or later.

And where had she failed as a mother? She had always been

open and honest with Kim about sex—and everything else, for that matter. She had tried to instill moral values in Kim—not a rigid set of "thou shalt nots" but some common sense and responsibility, and that didn't seem to have worked. Maybe she should have come down harder on Kim and forbidden her to date just Brandon. Or perhaps she should have been around more lately and not so involved with her job. But it probably would have happened no matter what Carol had or had not done.

Carol finished her cigarette and changed into a comfortable pair of walking shorts and a matching blouse. Kim was still holed up in her room, so Carol turned on the television in the breakfast area and prepared a simple broiled chicken dinner. She called Kim, and when Kim did not appear she knocked on her bedroom door.

"Honey, come on out and eat supper. I have chicken ready."

"I'm not hungry," Kim said.

Carol opened the door and stuck in her head. "You may not be, but your baby probably is," she said coaxingly. "One of the first rules of taking care of an unborn baby is to feed it properly. Come on, Kim. Try to eat a little."

"All right," Kim said woodenly as she pushed herself up off her bed. She followed Carol into the kitchen and put the smaller of the two chicken breasts onto her plate, along with small portions of beans and salad.

"I would have fixed steak, but I remember how sick it used to make me," Carol said as she sat down. "Are you feeling woozy in the morning yet?"

"A little," Kim admitted.

"Have you been to the doctor?" Carol asked.

"I went yesterday," Kim said tersely. She pointedly lowered her head and cut a piece of chicken.

Dinner was uncomfortable. Carol asked Kim a few questions, which Kim answered in monosyllables. She knew that Kim was hurt by her refusal to let her marry Brandon, and Carol hated hurting her daughter that way. But she had to think of what was good for Kim, and that wasn't marrying Brandon Stone at the age of seventeen.

Kim helped Carol clean up the kitchen and load the dishwasher as she usually did, and Carol could tell that the girl was about to escape to her room when the doorbell rang. She glanced at the clock. Harlan Stone had said that he and Brandon would be over at seven to talk. This afternoon she had been violently opposed to Harlan and his son having anything to do with Kim, but at this point she was almost relieved to hear from them. Maybe Harlan Stone could accomplish with Kim what she could not.

Kim peered out the door. "It's Brandon and Mr. Stone. Brandon!" she said as she stepped out on the porch and threw herself into Brandon's arms. "She says we can't get married!" The girl sobbed as she wrapped her arms around Brandon's waist. "She says she'll get the marriage annulled and send me to Aunt Margaret's in California."

Brandon shot Carol a dirty look as he cradled Kim. "Hush, honey, it's going to be all right," he crooned as Kim sobbed in his arms. "Why did you have to get her upset?" he demanded of Carol. "Don't you care anything about her?"

Carol stood in the door and crossed her arms in front of her. "Why did you have to get her pregnant?" she asked coldly. "Don't *you* care anything about her?"

Brandon's cheeks turned the same embarrassed shade of red that his father's had earlier that afternoon. "Yes, I care about her," he mumbled.

"Well, I'm glad we're all agreed that we care about Kim," Harlan said sardonically as he stood a few feet down the sidewalk, observing the scene impatiently. "Do you think we could go inside and talk about this?"

"Of course," Carol said. Brandon and Kim made no move toward the door, so Harlan stepped around them and brushed past Carol as he went into the house.

"Way to go, Mom," he said derisively as he gestured to the

embracing couple on the front porch. "Did a wonderful job there, didn't you?"

Carol shot him a frosty look as he sat down in a wing chair. "As I recall, you marched into my office and demanded that I do something about it, and I tried. You're the one who was so hell-bent on preventing your son from getting trapped. Why don't you see if you can do any better?"

Harlan glowered at her out from under thick, dark eyebrows. "I just might," he said, pulling his ankle up over his knee. As he stared out the front door at Kim and Brandon, Carol took another look at the man who had invaded her office earlier today. If she had been paying attention to him this afternoon, she probably could have figured out who he was before he introduced himself. She could see where Brandon had inherited his dark good looks and his well-muscled body. Harlan was a striking man, tall and hard and lean, not an extra ounce of flesh on his rangy frame. The muscles bulged in his forearms and chest, and although the wrinkles around his eyes and the gray strands in his hair revealed that he was probably about forty, his hips were still lean and his stomach was as flat as his son's. His clothes were well worn but clean, the jeans fitting him like a second skin and revealing the taut muscles of his calves and thighs. Oh, yes, he was a magnificent specimen of the male animal, this Harlan Stone, and if circumstances had been different—if he had been different—she could have been very much attracted to him.

Carol lowered her eyes as Harlan's gaze left the open door. She could feel his eyes scrutinizing her as she had studied him. As she looked up, their eyes met, and suddenly they were staring, aware of each other not as adversaries but as two human beings, a man and a woman.

Carol was the first to break the stare. "Kim! Brandon!" she called as she tore her eyes away from Harlan's. "Come on in here, please."

Brandon and Kim walked hand in hand into the living room and sat down across from them on the couch.

"Mrs. Venson, I'm sorry that I got Kim into trouble," Brandon said as he put his arm around Kim. "But I do love her, which is why we did what we did, and I want to marry her. And it isn't just because of the baby," he added. "I had already asked Kim to marry me someday before we were, well . . ."

"We love each other, Mom," Kim said. "That's what I tried to tell you earlier. But you just wouldn't listen."

Carol crossed her legs and clasped her hands in front of her. "Brandon, your father and I are both opposed to you getting married right now," she began.

"That's not what Dad said on the way over here," Brandon replied quickly.

Carol looked over at Harlan in surprise and raised her eyebrows. "This afternoon you were determined not to let this marriage take place," she said. "Would you care to tell Brandon and Kim what you told me?"

"I've reconsidered since we spoke this afternoon," Harlan said. "Although I must admit that I'm not thrilled, I'm not so sure that this marriage would be such a bad thing if Kim and Brand really do love each other."

"You've *what?*" she cried. Carol simply couldn't hide the horror she felt.

"I said I've reconsidered," Harlan said patiently. "I don't think this marriage would necessarily be such a bad thing."

"Well, I do!" Carol snapped. "What made you change your mind, Mr. Stone? Did you drive up and get a good look at the house and the cars in front of it? Did you decide that maybe Brandon was onto a good thing here? And to think you had the nerve to accuse Kim of being a golddigger!"

"Mother!" Kim cried, horrified.

"Dad, did you really say that?" Brandon asked.

"Yes, he most certainly did," Carol replied before Harlan could.

"I said I was sorry!" Harlan exclaimed. "And I think you owe me an apology for those little cracks of yours."

"You're not going to get one," Carol told him. "What am I

supposed to think? You come into my office breathing fire, and three hours later you're singing an altogether different tune. What made you change your mind so fast?"

"This isn't getting us anywhere," Brandon broke in. "Mrs. Venson, I'm not a golddigger. I wouldn't expect any help from you, and I'd refuse it if you offered. I'm not rich, but Dad pays me well and I can afford to support your daughter."

"How well?" Carol asked. "And I'm not asking to be nasty. I really would like to know just how well you think you could take care of her."

"She wouldn't starve," Harlan said sardonically.

"And how long would you continue to work for your father?" Carol asked.

"I hope to either inherit or buy the business from him someday," Brandon said.

"That's my point." Carol stopped and took a breath. "Brandon, Mr. Stone, I'm going to tell you exactly what I told Kim this afternoon. Kim's starting college this fall. She has the potential to become a professional woman or a businesswoman someday. And she simply deserves better in life than to be married to a common laborer, even if she wouldn't starve with him."

"Mother," Kim said, horrified, "you're terrible!"

"No, I appreciate your mother's honesty," Harlan said coldly. "Because it gives me a chance to set her straight on a few points. First off, Brandon and I are not common laborers. I happen to own a small business, complete with a hefty investment in equipment, seven trimmers, and a bookkeeper. Brandon will inherit that business someday. Admittedly, we don't live like this, Mrs. Venson, but I don't think it will hurt Kim if she has to drive a simple car instead of a fancy one like yours."

"You still don't understand what I'm trying to say," Carol said quietly. "I apologize for calling you common laborers. I'm sure you earn an adequate living. But in ten years Kim is going to have outgrown Brandon, if the marriage even lasts that long. She's going to have been to college, she'll have grown tremendously as a person and hopefully be started in a career of some sort. And Brandon will still be trimming trees. Look, if I thought the marriage had any chance at all, I'd say sure. But under these circumstances I can't see any point in agreeing to it. I'm sorry, but I simply refuse to go along with it."

Kim and Brandon looked at one another. "I guess we wait until November," Brandon said softly. "We'll marry right after your birthday."

"All right," Kim said.

"You're going to be mighty pregnant at your wedding," Brandon teased as he tightened his arm around her. "All right, Mrs. Venson, we'll do it your way. I'll marry her in November."

"Please, why won't you two listen to some sense?" Carol snapped as she glared at Kim and Brandon. "Look, Brandon, I'm not just trying to play the heavy. I've been there! I'm only thirty-seven years old. I had to get married because of Kim, and it was miserable, almost ten years of hell. Jack was just as miserable as I was. I don't want that for Kim—or you either, for that matter. I'm not asking you not to be a part of the baby's life. You could have the same privileges that a divorced father would have. Just please don't get married!"

"Don't mess up your daughter's life by marrying her, you mean," Brandon said bitterly.

"Yes, that's exactly what I mean," Carol said.

"Have you ever thought that the marriage wouldn't necessarily be miserable?" Harlan asked calmly.

"Of course it would be miserable," Carol said. "At their ages? It wouldn't work even if she weren't pregnant."

"Oh, I don't know," Harlan said softly. "Wanda and I got married while we were still in high school, and we were very happy."

"But did you have to?" Carol demanded.

"No, but we still had our share of problems, some of the same ones that Kim and Brand will be facing."

"Are you still together?" Carol asked pointedly. "I had the impression your household was all male."

"Wanda died eight years ago from cancer," Harlan said. "And it took Brandon and me a long time to get over her. I honestly can say our marriage would have made it for a lifetime, Mrs. Venson. I can understand why you're so hell-bent against this marriage, if your own was so bad, but all young marriages aren't that way. Some of them are very happy."

"But how can you be so sure that the two of them will be happy?" Carol asked. "They're so different!"

"Not all that different, Mom," Kim said. "Brandon may not be in college, but he's intelligent, and he probably reads more than we do."

"I'm not a stupid person, Mrs. Venson. I'm smart enough to know that I don't want my child to be illegitimate. Some people still care about that, and I'm one of them. Kim and I are going to get married. Now or in November, it really doesn't matter that much to me."

Carol looked from Brandon to Kim. They were determined, both of them. Apparently, real love had grown between the two young people during the last months, and she knew better than to think they would be over it by November. On the contrary, if she tried to keep them apart they would be just that much more determined to get married when Kim's birthday did arrive. Carol desperately wished she had nipped this thing in the bud when Brandon had started coming around, but it was too late to do anything now. She glanced over at Harlan and saw from the shrug he gave her that the decision was hers.

"All right. Marry him, Kim, if you must. Go get the calendar in the kitchen and you and Brandon can pick out a date."

"Oh, Mom, thank you!" Kim said as she jumped up and hugged her mother's neck. "We'll make it work, I promise you." She quickly brought a small calendar out to the living room and she and Brandon bent over it together. "What do you think of the third?" Kim asked Brandon earnestly.

"Touching," Harlan murmured to Carol.

Carol shot him a dirty look. "This is all your fault," she

snapped quietly. "If you hadn't changed your mind, I could have talked them out of it."

Harlan rubbed his hand across his forehead. "No, you couldn't," he said softly. "That's why I changed my mind. Because I couldn't get him to see things my way."

"How about the third of June?" Kim asked. "That will give us two and a half weeks."

"That's fine," Carol said, momentarily shutting her mind to the amount of work that the wedding was going to entail. "Six in the evening? You can marry at the church and I'll have a buffet catered here."

"That sounds good to me," Kim said.

"And we'll supply the kegs," Brandon said enthusiastically.

Carol couldn't suppress the small shudder that went through her. "That's all right, Brandon, we'll have plenty of beer at the bar." She happened to glance over at Harlan and was infuriated by his amused expression.

"Seriously, Mrs. Venson, I'd be glad to help pay for the wedding," Harlan said.

"No, I'd rather make the arrangements myself," Carol said quickly. "It will be easier on me than having to hassle with who pays for what."

"As you wish," Harlan said stiffly.

Carol could tell that she had offended him by her curt refusal. "Look, I really meant what I said about it being easier on me," she said gently. "Why don't you help them with some furniture? It's horribly expensive these days."

"No thanks, Dad," Brandon said quickly. "We'll make it on our own. We don't need a handout."

"It wouldn't be a handout," Harlan said. "It would be a wedding present. Please."

"All right," Brandon said.

"And Kim can keep her car," Carol said. "I'll have the title transferred to her name."

Brandon shook his head quickly. "No, that's too much to give us," he said. "The wedding will be enough."

"Don't be ridiculous," Carol said. "The car's already Kim's. Besides, you're not going to be able to buy her a car at first, are you?"

"Well, no," Brandon said. "But I don't see why she needs one right away."

"To get to college, Brandon," Kim said.

"You won't need it since you won't be going," Brandon replied.

"Won't be going?" Carol and Kim said in unison.

"Brandon, I'm not going to drop out of school!" Kim said. "I'm just starting."

"But what about the baby?" Brandon asked. "Kim, I don't like the idea of your going to college. You're pregnant and you have to think of the baby. You can go next year."

"Brandon, I'm going to college!" Kim said.

"Yes, Brandon, she certainly is going to college," Carol said in a tone that startled all four of them. She had never in her life understood the meaning of the phrase "seeing red," but at this point she did. Her face was a study of pure fury. "I've agreed to a marriage that I don't want to see happen, but there is no way —I repeat—no way that Kim is going to drop out of college before she even starts! You're not going to deprive her of her education." Carol stood up and paced the floor. "If you even think such a thing I'll have her on a plane to California so fast you won't know what happened." She poked her finger into the middle of Brandon's chest. "Do you understand that, young man?"

"Uh, yes, ma'am," Brandon stammered.

"Furthermore, you're going to promise me that you'll see Kim through to her degree—you'll either pay the tuition yourself or let me do it. None of this going-back-later nonsense."

"Don't you think you're going a little too far?" Harlan demanded.

Carol whirled around. "You stay out of this," she warned. "Now, Brandon, will you promise me that Kim gets her degree, or do I call the whole thing off?"

"Kim, I promise," Brandon mumbled.

"No, Brandon, you promise me, not her. Promises to wives have a way of being broken," she said bitterly.

"I promise, Mrs. Venson," Brandon said stiffly. "I'll see that she gets her degree." He turned to Kim. "Want to go out for a few minutes?" he asked. "I'll buy you a milkshake."

"Mom, is it all right?" Kim asked.

"Sure, hon, go ahead," Carol said as she sat back down in her chair, trembling in the aftermath of her anger. "Don't be too late."

Brandon and Kimberly escaped out the front door, and Carol picked up a pack of cigarettes and withdrew one with fingers that trembled. "Smoke?" she asked as she offered Harlan the pack.

Harlan took a cigarette and lit both his and hers. "They're not even married yet and you're already interfering," he said coldly.

"You're damn right I interfered. I did what I had to do," Carol said.

"You know, Mrs. Venson, you're quite a snob where that girl's concerned," Harlan said. "All this about her going to college and Brandon not being good enough for her. Most mothers would be grateful for a decent son-in-law who would treat their girl well."

"As you said, I'm a snob about her," Carol replied coolly. "Very much so. Now, about the wedding. It's going to have to be small." She glanced around her spacious living room. "Does thirty each sound fair? I'm sorry it can't be bigger, but I would dread trying to get a reception room on such short notice."

"I'm sure thirty will be fine."

Carol walked Harlan to the front door.

"Mrs. Venson, I'm sorry all this had to happen," he said. "I want you to know that I'm just as worried and upset about this as you are."

Tears glistened in Carol's eyes as she looked into his tired ones. "Yes, I know," she said. She felt a sudden warmth for this man, an empathy with him in the pain and disappointment they shared that night. In spite of her anger with him and his son, she wanted to reach out and run her hand down the side of his face and tell him that it was going to be all right. She was drawn to Harlan Stone in a way she didn't understand. Ruthlessly, she stifled her emotions, willing her feelings of warmth and attraction to go away. "Can you get me your list by the day after tomorrow?" she asked.

Harlan nodded. "Good night," he said as he left.

Carol shut the door behind him and sat down to make out her invitation list. Without her meaning to, she thought about a pair of bright-blue eyes staring at her from under thick black brows, and wondered what they would look like if they were smiling. She frowned when she realized where her thoughts were leading and sat down at her desk in the den. She had a lot to do in the next two and a half weeks, and she didn't have a moment to waste.

Harlan got into his car and fought his way across Houston in the heavy evening traffic. Carol Venson was an attractive woman, there was no doubt about that. A little too thin, maybe, but otherwise not bad at all. Harlan had dated women since his wife's death, but he hadn't felt this kind of attraction for a woman since he had seen Wanda for the first time all those years ago.

But physical attraction was as far as it went. Harlan turned on his blinker and got off the expressway at the exit closest to his home. Carol Venson might have been an attractive woman, but she was just about the biggest snob he had ever met, and she apparently was arrogant enough not to care that she was a snob. Most mothers would have been grateful that Brandon was more than willing to get married and wasn't trying to duck out on his responsibilities. But that wasn't good enough for Mrs. high-and-mighty Venson. No, she wanted a degree behind the name. Well, tough. She could take her aspirations for her daughter and go jump in the ship channel for all he cared. He had no use for someone like her.

CHAPTER THREE

Carol flinched at the harsh sound of the alarm clock. Fumbling a little, she slapped the buzzer off, and when she remembered what day it was she buried her head under the pillow, determined to postpone getting up. Kim and Brandon were getting married that day, and Carol knew that once she did get up, she would not have a moment's peace until late that night. She had dreaded this day for the last two and a half weeks, hoping all along that something would take place to discourage Kim or Brandon and change their minds. But the two young people were as determined to get married as they had been last month, so Carol, with a little help from Kim, had put together a simple wedding and reception, and at six o'clock this evening Kimberly would become Mrs. Brandon Stone.

Carol lay still for a few minutes, tired from all the preparations yet too anxious to go back to sleep. When she heard the sound of the shower in the front bathroom, she sat up and got out of bed. She stumbled groggily to her own bathroom and showered and washed her hair before she put on a pair of shorts and a T-shirt. This was Kim's last morning in this house, and Carol wanted them to have breakfast together one last time. As she had several times in the last two weeks, Carol realized that she would be alone now, and a lump formed in her throat. It was wrong, she silently raged, it was too soon; Kim should stay with her and not marry Brandon, but she knew that it wouldn't do any good even if she said the words out loud.

By the time Kim finally made it to the kitchen, Carol had

made scrambled eggs and a plate of toast. Kim sat down and put her head in her hands.

"Feeling rocky again?" Carol asked gently as she poured a glass of milk.

Kim nodded. "How long is this going to last?" she muttered as she picked up a piece of unbuttered toast and nibbled on it.

"Not much longer," Carol assured her as she gave the milk to Kim and poured herself a cup of tea before sitting down. "It should be over in another couple of weeks or so."

"No wonder you had just me," Kim said. "I'll never go through this again." She cautiously sipped her milk.

"It will get better, I promise," Carol said gently. "Pretty soon the nausea will be a dim memory." She blew on her hot tea and sipped it. "You know, I hate to say it, but you've been a lot sicker than I ever was. I really didn't feel as bad as you do."

"I'm glad. I wouldn't wish this on my worst enemy."

"Not even Brandon?" Carol teased, winking.

Kim grinned weakly. "Well, there are days." She ate some eggs and swallowed some more milk.

At that moment the telephone rang, and Carol reached over to the counter to pick up the extension. "Hello? Oh, good morning, Brandon. Yes, she's here, but you can't speak to her. Why not? Don't you know that it's bad luck to talk to your bride on your wedding day? Yes, Brandon, telephones count." She winked at Kim, who was trying to smother her laughter. "Of course you can speak to her, Brandon. Just don't keep her too long. We have a lot to do today." She handed the telephone to Kim and cleared the breakfast dishes before tackling the last details of the wedding.

In the early afternoon, a few of Carol's relatives started arriving in town, either calling from their hotel rooms for directions to the church, or dropping by the house for a few minutes. Kimberly helped for a while, but she began to tire and Carol sent her to her room to rest. Carol was getting more frantic by the minute, and when her parents finally arrived around four they found her tired and snappish.

"I swear I didn't know there was so much to do before a wedding," Carol said as she opened her arms to her mother.

Ada and Jerry Follis hugged their eldest daughter. "I remember how it was when we got yours ready in such a hurry," Ada said as she bustled in, Jerry following her quietly. "Land sakes, Carol, it didn't have to be this fancy! You've knocked yourself out."

Carol smiled weakly. "You planned a nice one for me on short notice," she reminded Ada.

Ada looked at Carol shrewdly. "Same reason?" she asked.

Carol nodded, cringing inwardly at the disappointment that Ada and Jerry couldn't hide. "I'm sorry, Mama. I did the best I could with her."

"Don't blame yourself, Carol," Ada said gently. "It wasn't your fault, any more than it was ours when it happened to you." Ada couldn't hold back a sigh. "But I can't help feeling badly about it. I so hoped she would get to have all the fun that you never had as a girl."

"So did I, Mama," Carol admitted.

"Now. You look like you're about to drop," Ada said briskly as she observed her daughter's tired face. "And I'd put money on the fact that your stomach's acting up. You go rest awhile, and I'll answer the phone and the doorbell."

"Thanks," Carol said as she trudged to the back of the house. She took her ulcer medication and jerked off her rumpled shorts and T-shirt and lay down on the bed, closing her eyes as she waited for the medication to take effect. Her parents had tried, but they had not been able to hide their disappointment. Though Ada had admonished Carol not to blame herself, she knew that deep down, her parents were bound to hold her just a little responsible. How could they help it? She was Kim's mother. And although Ada would bite her tongue out before she said it out loud, one of her favorite quotations had always been "Like mother, like daughter." Carol had made a mistake and gotten pregnant out of wedlock, and her daughter had done the same. Oh, the circumstances were a little different, but

Kim's situation was basically the same that hers had been eighteen years ago.

For the first time in a long while, Carol's thoughts drifted back to the past, to her freshman year at the University of Texas. It was during the sixties, and Carol had been caught up in the freedom and the rebellion of the era. Seduced by both the freedom of the times and the handsome senior, it didn't take Carol long to abandon her family's strict moral principles and end up in Jack Venson's bed.

Carol had been horrified when she found out about the baby. Jack had been furious, revealing for the first time a nasty streak that seemed to get worse the longer they were together, but in the end he agreed to marry her. After Kim's birth, Carol had wanted to go back to school, but Jack's starting salary as an engineer would not pay for both tuition and child care, so Carol put her own dreams on hold and poured her love and energy into her small daughter.

Jack's career prospered, but the marriage went rapidly downhill, with noisy fights and tense silences. Carol would have loved to have walked out, but she had no skills and could not have supported her daughter. Although Jack did not particularly love Carol, he did feel responsible for her and Kim, so he did not leave, either.

Determined to get her degree, Carol went back to college the year Kimberly started first grade. In spite of Jack's lack of cooperation, she made it through her classes with respectable grades and tried to ignore the long evenings and weekends when Jack did not come home. She knew her marriage was destined to fail, that it was just a matter of time, but at that point all she cared about was getting her degree so she could support Kim. Jack stuck it out until the middle of Carol's junior year, and a sympathetic judge awarded the bulk of their joint bank account, such as it was, to her. By scrimping and economizing on everything, Carol had managed to make it through and graduate.

Carol sighed as she stared up at the ceiling. She had wasted almost ten miserable years with Jack, and she had not been able to start her career until she had reached the age of thirty. Now her biggest fear was that the same thing would happen to Kim. She silently damned Brandon for getting Kim into this mess and his father for supporting the marriage. She hoped Harlan Stone was as worried as she was this afternoon! Sighing, Carol made a face as she looked at the clock. She climbed off her bed and picked up the fresh lingerie she had laid out on her dresser earlier in the day.

Forty-five minutes later Carol stood in front of the full-length mirror and stared at her reflection critically. She was a little young to be the mother of the bride, that was for sure! She had passed up the dowdy selections in the wedding shop and had chosen instead a drop-waist sheath in a lovely rose silk that enchanced her creamy complexion. The dress's neckline plunged somewhat, revealing the barest hint of Carol's cleavage, but its petaled sleeves saved the dress from anything but the slightest hint of provocation. Carol leaned into the mirror and peered at the deep circles under her eyes that she couldn't quite hide with makeup. The wedding had been a lot of work, and she had not slept well the last few nights, her worries about Kim keeping her awake long after her head had hit the pillow.

Carol picked up her purse and knocked on the door of Kim's room.

"Is that you, Mother?" Kim called out.

Carol pushed open the door. Kim was sitting at her dressing table in her bra and slip, her hair a tangle of uncombed curls.

"Need any help?" she asked.

"I can't get my hair up," Kimberly admitted as she struggled to control the heavy waves that slipped through her fingers.

"Here, let me," Carol said as she picked up Kim's brush. Carol had worn her hair long for years before she had finally had it cut, and knew how to manage it. In just a few minutes she had piled Kim's hair on the top of her head in a puffy Gibson Girl. "Did you pack the things I left in here last night?" she asked.

"Yes. I meant to thank you for them, but I was a little emba rassed," Kim admitted. Carol had bought Kim several love nightgowns and a practical, no-nonsense marriage manu along with a vacuum cleaner and a television set. "They're r ally lovely, Mom."

"I'm glad you like them," Carol said. "Did you read th book?"

Kim blushed. "Yes. Thanks. It was a lot of help, even thoug I—we. . . ."

"I wish somebody had given me one," Carol said honestl She sat down on Kim's bed. "Kim, I want you to promise m that you and Brandon will do everything you can to make you marriage work," she said quietly. "I know I opposed you first, but if he's the young man of your choice, then I wish yo both the best."

"Do you mean that?" Kimberly asked.

"Yes, I do. I love you, and I'll learn to love him, because yo chose him."

"Thanks, Mom," Kimberly said, her eyes filling with happ tears. "We'll make this marriage work. I promise."

"Come on, Kim," Carol said huskily, "let's get you into you dress."

Carol helped Kim into her wedding dress, blinking back tear at the sight of the beautiful young woman who was her daugh ter, and Ada and Jerry joined them on the short drive to th church. Since Jack had refused to come to the wedding unde the circumstances, Jerry had agreed to give Kimberly away Carol's stomach was churning and her hands were tremblin almost as much as Kim's when they entered the church parlo to wait for the signal that it was time to begin. By the time th photographer had taken some portraits, Carol's stomach wa hurting badly, so she cheated and took a dose of medicine ear lier than she was supposed to.

Harlan knocked on the door before he stuck his head in. "I everybody ready?" he asked as he looked around at the tense nervous faces in the parlor. Carol stared at him, unable to hid her amazement at the difference in him that night. When she had seen him before, he had been dressed in jeans, and he had been rugged and appealing in an earthy way. But tonight he looked handsome and refined in his tuxedo, and Carol was amazed at the purely sensual attraction she felt for him. She saw Harlan's gaze linger on her for a moment and felt the heat rise in her face.

Harlan found it difficult to take his eyes off Carol Venson. If he had been attracted to her before, in her business suit and her shorts, he was positively bowled over as he stared at her in her rose dress. He might have known she wouldn't wear a sedate mother-of-the-bride outfit! The silky material clung to her bodice and swirled around her legs, drawing his eyes up and down her womanly body. As his gaze was drawn to Carol's tired face, he paused. Though she had been violently opposed to this marriage, she had knocked herself out to get the wedding ready for the kids. For the first time he felt a flicker of admiration for the woman behind the beautiful face and appealing body.

"Shouldn't you be with Brandon?" Carol asked as the wedding party entered the foyer. "I thought you were going to be the best man."

"Brandon decided that I would look out of place walking with Chrissi," Harlan said dryly as he gestured toward the young maid of honor. "I was just as glad when he asked his best friend." Carol murmured something noncommittal as the organ music began. Harlan escorted Brandon's grandmother in and one of Brandon's friends took Carol down the aisle.

The wedding was simple, subdued, but very beautiful. Carol's eyes brimmed with tears several times during the ceremony, but she managed to keep them from falling, and during the wedding prayer she prayed fervently that Kim's marriage would be better than her own had been. After the ceremony the photographer quickly snapped the posed photographs, and within an hour they were back at Carol's house, where the caterers waited with a delicious buffet for the wedding party and guests.

Since Brandon and Kim had not wanted a receiving line,

preferring to mingle with their guests, the caterers began serving immediately. Carol checked with the chef in the kitchen, who assured her that everything was going well and suggested politely that she leave everything to them. She was hurrying back to the party when she collided with Harlan in the kitchen doorway.

"Oh, I'm sorry, Harlan," she stammered as his strong hands reached out and gripped her shoulders. She could feel the warmth of his body through the tuxedo and could smell his tangy aftershave. "I wasn't looking where I was going."

"That's all right," Harlan said as he released her shoulders. He smiled, really smiled at her, and Carol could feel her insides melting.

"Were you looking for anything in particular?" Carol asked.

"No, not really," he responded. "My mother insisted that I check and see if you needed some help in the kitchen. She's not used to these catered things."

"That's kind of her, but they seem to have everything under control," Carol said. "In fact, they more or less shooed me out. Why don't you introduce me to your mother, so I can thank her for her offer?"

Harlan took Carol's arm and escorted her across the room to his mother, who was standing in the corner talking with another of Brandon's relatives. "Mom, this is Kimberly's mother," he said to the sweet-faced woman who had accompanied him at the wedding. "My mother, Joyce Stone."

Carol extended her hand. "Hello, Mrs. Stone, it's nice to meet you. I wanted to thank you for sending your son to the kitchen to see if we needed help."

"You're welcome," Mrs. Stone said shyly. "Is there anything I can do? You've worked so hard on everything."

"Well, right now the caterers have everything under control," Carol said. "But I won't hesitate to call on you later if I need you."

"I'd be glad to help," Mrs. Stone said. She fell silent, she and the other woman gazing around at Carol's family room uneasily.

Carol extended her hand to the other woman. "I don't believe we've met," she said. "I'm Carol Venson."

"I'm Mattie Hughes," she said as she shook Carol's outstretched hand. "Brandon's aunt. Your home's mighty pretty, Mrs. Venson."

"Why, thank you," Carol said as she gazed around her family room and into the crowded living room. "I've enjoyed living here."

Carol talked with Brandon's grandmother and aunt for a few more minutes, but she could tell that they were ill at ease around her. She visited with a few more of his relatives, all of whom were very nice, but Carol could tell they felt just as uneasy around her as Mrs. Stone had. Puzzled, she spotted her attorney, a man she sometimes dated, Scott Ryan, having a drink with her father at the bar.

"Everything's going beautifully, Carol," Jerry said as she approached the two men.

"If everything's going so well, why are my guests all in the living room and the Stone's guests all in the family room?" Carol asked dryly. "I tried to mingle, but they were all so uncomfortable around me it made me wonder if I had done something to offend them."

Scott straighted up and grinned lazily. "Carol, for a sophisticated lady, sometimes you can certainly be naive. You and this house intimidate them."

"Intimidate them?" Carol asked. "Do you really think that's what it is?"

"Of course it is," Scott said as he sipped his drink, wicked amusement dancing in his eyes.

"Carol, honey, Scott's probably right," Jerry said gently. "You forget that everybody doesn't live the way you do."

Carol eyed the crowd in the living room. "I guess you're right," she said. "I wonder what Kim's going to think of Brandon's relatives."

"She'll probably have an easier time accepting them than you will," Scott said as he shook his finger at her playfully. "Go eat. You look hungry."

Carol filled a plate and sat down beside her cousin, who pumped Carol unmercifully on the stock market. The minute she was finished eating, she escaped gratefully with her empty plate to the kitchen and checked with the caterers, who assured her that there would be plenty of food. The bar, however, was running short of Scotch and mixers. Carol glanced into the family room. Spotting Scott and her father talking with Harlan, she got some cash out of her purse and folded it into her hand. "Excuse me," she said as she neared them. "Scott, would you mind running down to the liquor store? I'm almost out of Scotch and most of the mixers."

"Do you want me to get them?" Harlan offered quickly.

"No, that's all right, I'll go," Scott said cheerfully. "See you in a little while."

"Thank you, though," Carol said to Harlan as Scott left the room.

"I think your friend is amused by this whole thing," he said dryly.

Carol's face burned. "Yes, he is," she said quietly. "Scott's a bachelor. He doesn't know what it's like to worry about a child."

"Well, I'm considerably less worried than I was at first," Harlan said to both Carol and her father. "I think Kim's a lovely young woman and I'm glad she's going to be part of our family."

Jerry smiled. "Thank you, Mr. Stone," he said. "I'm sure Carol feels the same way about Brandon."

Harlan turned sardonic eyes on Carol, who swallowed guiltily. "Brandon's a nice young man," she said quietly. "Very polite and kind. I've always thought that."

As Jerry was called away by his wife, Harlan taunted softly. "But that's not enough for you, is it?"

"Not tonight, Harlan," Carol said through clenched teeth as

she started to turn away, but she stiffened as she saw who was coming through the front door. "He said he wasn't coming," she ground out.

Harlan watched the tall, good-looking blond man walk into the room with a slender redhead at his side. "Kim's father?" he asked. He could feel Carol's intense dislike for the man.

Carol nodded. "He wouldn't come to the church and give her away, but he feels free to waltz in here," she said angrily. "That's just like Jack."

Harlan watched with narrowed eyes as Jack Venson enveloped his daughter in a theatrical embrace and shook Brandon's hand.

"Pompous hypocrite," Carol fumed. "He wouldn't even speak to her before the wedding. Excuse me, Harlan, I guess I better go speak to the jerk." She forced herself to look pleasant and made her way through the crowded room to where Jack and Leslie, the woman he had married last year, were standing.

Carol had almost reached them when she realized that Harlan had come with her. "Introduce me to him," Harlan said.

"If you like," Carol said tiredly. Ada and Jerry had spotted Jack too, and her mother's lips had thinned at the sight of the man who had made her daughter so miserable for so many years. Carol forced herself to keep her smile in place as she extended her hand to Jack. "Hello, Jack. I'm glad you and Leslie could make it after all."

"Wouldn't want to miss my daughter's nuptial party," Jack said as he shook Carol's hand. "You're looking as beautiful as ever, Carol."

"Thank you. You're looking well too. And Leslie, it's good to see you again." Carol had met Kim's stepmother on one other occasion and found her a surprisingly nice person.

"Thank you, it's good to see you too," Leslie said. "Kim looks beautiful, doesn't she?"

Carol glanced over at her daughter. "Yes, she does."

"At least she isn't showing yet," Jack said quietly. Carol

flinched and Harlan gripped her arm reassuringly. "I'd like to get my hands on that bastard boy's neck and wring it," Jack continued.

"That's my bastard boy you're talking about," Harlan said smilingly, "and I'd prefer that you leave his neck alone. I understand from Carol and Kim that you're a fine one to talk."

Jack's face turned a dull shade of red. "I'm just concerned about my daughter," he blustered as he extended his hand. "I'm Jack Venson."

"Harlan Stone." Harlan shook Jack's hand, gripping it just a fraction too tightly.

"Jack, Leslie, would you like something to eat or drink?" Carol broke in quickly. "The buffet's in the dining room and the bar's set up out on the patio."

"Yes, that sounds great," Leslie said. "Come on, Jack." She started toward the buffet table, but Jack remained with Carol and Harlan.

"Coming," Jack said. "Anyway, Carol, for such short notice you did your usual magnificent job on Kim's reception. It's a shame you didn't do that good a job of raising her."

Carol's face burned. "I think I did a pretty good job in spite of this," she said hotly. "Considering the fact that I had to do it without any help from you. Leslie's waiting, Jack."

Jack followed Leslie to the buffet table, leaving Harlan and Carol in the middle of the room. "Is he always such a bastard?" Harlan asked.

"No, only when he's around me," Carol admitted. "I just seem to bring out the worst in him. And he does it to me—I turn into an absolute shrew around him."

"That's too bad," Harlan said. "Why do you two affect each other like that?"

"Well," Carol said with a sigh, "by the time we decided to put an end to our marriage, we thoroughly despised one another. There are a lot of things neither one of us can forgive."

"But you've been divorced almost ten years," Harlan said. "Surely the ill feelings have faded a little by now, haven't they?"

"That's the sad part," she replied. "They have. This is mild compared to the way we used to be." She stopped and took a deep breath. "Would you like another drink or something else to eat?"

"I'm fine," Harlan said. "Have you met my brother-in-law yet?" He gestured to his late wife's brother and introduced Carol to him.

A short time later Carol checked her watch and suggested to Brandon and Kim that they go ahead and cut the cake, in case some of their guests had to leave soon. They shared a bite for the photographer and Kim threw her bouquet after Brandon tossed the garter. As Jack made a production of toasting the young couple and giving them a check for their honeymoon, Carol seethed inwardly, thinking of all she had spent on the wedding and Harlan had spent on furniture. She caught the look in Harlan's eye and knew he was thinking the same thing. As soon as he had a chance, Harlan took Jack aside, and a few minutes later a red-faced Jack hustled Leslie out the door without even saying good-bye. Carol would have loved to have known what Harlan said to make him leave like that! Her eyes dancing wickedly, she started across the room toward Harlan, but at that moment Kim and Brandon reappeared in their traveling clothes and motioned to Carol and Harlan.

"Thanks, Mrs. Venson, Dad," Brandon said as he shook Harlan's hand. Unashamed, Harlan enveloped his son in a hug.

"Mom, thanks for everything," Kim said. "We couldn't have asked for a nicer wedding." She turned to Harlan. "I'll be good to him, Mr. Stone."

Brandon took Carol's hand. "I'll keep that promise I made you," he assured her.

Carol hugged Brandon briefly. "Thanks," she said. "Have a good time at the coast."

Kim and Brandon ran out the door, their friends in hot pursuit, flinging rice and laughing happily.

It was another hour before the wedding guests finally left the house. Kim and Brandon's friends seemed determined to eat the buffet table bare, and Carol's relatives from out of town were glad for the chance to visit with one another and were reluctant to leave. By the time the last of her great-aunts had waved good-bye from the curb, Carol had a screaming headache, her stomach was a mess, and she was practically in tears from the emotional stress the day had wrought.

Rubbing her temples with the tips of her fingers, she returned to the kitchen and sat down at the table to write the caterers a check, trying to ignore the mess that awaited her. The caterers had done a good job of cleaning up after themselves in the kitchen, but the other rooms suffered from the usual aftermath of a party. Carol handed the check to the owner of the company, thanking him for the delicious buffet, and had kicked off her shoes and was rubbing one foot with the other when Harlan came into the kitchen and sat down across from her at the table.

"You still here?" Carol asked. "I thought you'd gone home by now."

"No, I want to stay and help you clean up a little," Harlan said. "Unless your maid will come in and do it for you tomorrow."

"I don't have a maid," Carol admitted. "I have a thing about having someone in my house while I'm gone." She stood up, not bothering to put her shoes back on. "I'll take you up on your offer, if you really don't mind helping me. I'm exhausted, but leaving it until tomorrow would be worse."

"No, I'm glad to help out," Harlan said as he picked up the freshly lined garbage pail and carried it into the family room. Her head pounding, Carol started stacking the dirty cups and plates while Harlan gathered up the napkins and highball glasses.

"That was one of the nicest weddings and receptions I've ever attended. You did a great job," Harlan volunteered.

Carol smiled faintly as she carried a stack of plates into the kitchen. "Thanks," she called through the open door. "I just wanted it to be nice for them. Did your family have a good time?"

"I think so," Harlan said. "They all knew the circumstances, though, and they're worried."

Carol returned to the family room and started another stack of plates. "I didn't try to hide it, either," she admitted. "I remember how Mother pretended that we had fallen madly in love and later she tried to pass Kim off as premature. Have you ever seen a preemie that weighed almost eight pounds?"

"Wanda and I skipped all this," Harlan said as he tossed a dirty napkin into the trash. "We ran off, and I think Wanda always felt cheated because she didn't get a church wedding."

"I'm sorry I went to mine," Carol admitted. "I would have been better off having Kim alone. Young marriages just don't work, especially if they're shotgun." Tears clouded her eyes as she thought of Kim, and she didn't see the way Harlan's eyes narrowed. "I'm afraid this one isn't going to be any different."

"Keep talking like that and you'll push them into a divorce," Harlan snapped angrily. "What is it with you? Young marriages can work. I swear to God, I think you want that marriage to fail so you can pick her out a husband who meets your specifications!"

Carol paused as the tears that had been threatening to fall spilled over onto her cheeks. "How can you say a thing like that?" she whispered before the first sob tore through her. She dropped the plate she was holding, not noticing when it hit the floor and shattered in every direction. Burying her face in her hands, she finally gave in to the tension and worry and disappointment she had tried so hard to deal with. Harsh sobs racked her body as she shook her head back and forth.

She immediately felt herself being enveloped by a pair of strong, warm arms. "Oh, Carol, I'm sorry," Harlan said as he pushed her head down on his shoulder. "I should never have said that."

Carol tried to stem the flow of tears from her eyes, but they seemed to have a will of their own. "How—how could you think that I want my daughter's marriage to fail?" She sobbed into his shoulder. "Do you have any idea how painful a divorce is? Do you really think I want that for her?"

"I'm sorry, I'm sorry," Harlan crooned over and over. Before Carol realized what was happening, she felt Harlan's strong arms leading her to the couch, where he sat beside her. He said nothing more, but just let her pour out her emotions until she was spent.

Carol sniffed and raised her head, blowing her nose on a clean napkin she found on the end table. "Please, Harlan, don't ever think I want that marriage to end," she said. "You saw Jack and me tonight. I don't want Kim to despise the father of her child or know the pain of a broken marriage. I don't want her to have to walk away from the divorce court with that awful sense of failure."

Harlan reached up and wiped the tears from Carol's cheeks. "I'm sorry, Carol. I was wrong to think you felt that way. But I know that Brandon isn't the kind of man you wanted for her."

"That's true, but Kim has made her choice," Carol said as Harlan's fingers trailed down her cheek to her chin. "And if Brandon is the one, I hope and pray they'll be happy."

"Thanks," Harlan whispered, his fingers lightly touching her lips. Carol stared into Harlan's eyes, mesmerized by the blue fire she saw there, and it seemed perfectly natural to sway toward him just a little. Harlan's hands found their way to her shoulders and ever so slowly he pulled her to him.

Their mouths met, softly at first, as Harlan tenderly explored the delicate skin of her lips. His touch was warm and comforting as he sought to let his kiss and his touch reassure Carol that everything was going to be all right. She responded by parting her lips ever so slightly, welcoming his gentle compassion. Their lips touched and teased as they shared an exquisite moment, then Harlan held her face between his hands and brought his lips firmly against hers.

Still guided more by comfort than passion, Harlan kissed Carol for a long time, his lips gently coaxing hers open as he drank in her sweetness. Carol moaned as she moved closer to him, seeking the warmth and reassurance she so desperately craved. She could feel the tips of her breasts brushing against his chest, and when she laid her hand against him she could feel his heart pounding. Her own pulse was soaring, and when Harlan tried to pull away she put her arms around his neck to keep him close. Her comfort turning into desire, she shivered, knowing she had to stop yet not quite having the strength to do so.

Harlan gasped slightly when Carol pulled him closer to her and refused to let him go. He had tried to do the gentlemanly thing and pull away from her, knowing that his caress of comfort was turning into something more, but when he realized that Carol was as attracted to him as he was to her, he gave up and let himself be guided by his feelings for the beautiful woman he held in his arms. His hands massaged the soft, tender flesh of her back. She was a small woman, fragile and precious, although the arms that circled his neck and held him tightly were anything but weak.

They kissed and caressed one another, each letting go for a few delicious minutes of madness before Carol finally realized who she was kissing and pulled away, her face burning with embarrassment. Harlan took a deep breath as he ran his hand down the side of her rosy cheek.

"I'm sorry, Carol," he said as he pulled away from her. "You were upset and I took advantage of you."

"It wasn't like that," Carol replied softly. "We both . . . we both needed that kiss."

Harlan nodded as he got up off the couch. "Don't get up until I get the glass swept up," he told her. Then he brought a broom and a dustpan from the utility room and Carol's shoes from the kitchen, and together they cleaned up the worst of the mess, working quickly and not speaking. Harlan took the last of the trash bags to the kitchen and wished Carol a quick, somewhat awkward good night.

Carol turned out the lights in the front of the house and escaped to a long, hot bath. She put on a nightgown and sat down in the chair beside her bed, lightly touching her lips with the tips of her fingers. How could she have responded to Harlan like that? A man with whom she had nothing in common except a powerful physical attraction? An embarrassed blush stained her cheeks once again. Oh, yes, she had to admit to herself that she found him physically attractive—that was the problem. They had nothing to offer each other except those elemental feelings, and for Carol that had never been enough.

Harlan locked his front door behind him and sat down on the couch in his living room. He glanced around at the comfortable room with the homey furniture, trying to see it through Carol's eyes. She would probably find it dull and shabby, compared with her elegant place. Still, Harlan liked the comfort of his home and appreciated the fact that he almost had it paid for. He took off the rented jacket, laying it carefully across the arm of the chair, and lit a cigarette as he thought about the kiss he had just shared and the woman with whom he had shared it.

Harlan admitted to himself that he was very attracted to Carol, more attracted to her than he had been to any woman since Wanda died, and if the way she kissed him back had been any indication, she felt the same way about him. Harlan didn't want to let go of that. He and Carol deserved to get to know each other better, to see if there was or could be anything between them besides a physical desire. He wanted to kiss her again and make love to her, but he also wanted to talk to her and find out what made her tick. Harlan realized that he was going to have a hard time convincing Carol to go out with him, to get to know him better. If her attitude toward Brandon was anything to go by, she'd be wary of him, suspicious of his high school diploma, his blue-collar job, and his moderate income. Harlan smiled grimly as he stubbed out his cigarette. He was going to have to work hard to overcome Carol Venson's prejudices. Well, that was all right; he had never been afraid of a little hard work.

CHAPTER FOUR

Carol balanced the telephone on her shoulder as she wrote out a ticket for one of Van Preston's clients.

"Sure, Kim, I'd love to come for dinner, if Brandon's willing to fight the traffic and pick me up," she said. "My car's in the shop overnight."

"Sure, Mom, no problem," Kim said cheerfully. "I'll have Sally buzz him on the pager. What would you like to eat?"

"Food!" Carol said enthusiastically. She had overslept and had forgotten to bring her lunch, and her stomach was beginning to feel empty. "Anything will be fine. Are you all set for registration next week?"

"Yes, and I can hardly wait," Kim enthused. "I never thought I'd be so excited about going to school."

"I'm glad," Carol said warmly. "There goes my other line, got to go. See you tonight."

Carol answered the other call, which proved to be brief, and finished the ticket she had been writing out. She was filling in this afternoon for one of her fellow stockbrokers and had gotten a message that one of his clients wanted to sell a thousand shares of Osso. Carol wondered why on earth anyone would want to sell a stock that was going up in value, but that was between Van and his client. She left her office and smiled as she handed the ticket to Bennie.

"Is Ronnie all packed and ready to go?" she asked.

"Yes. He's so excited he can hardly stand it," Bennie said proudly. "And how about Kim—is she ready to start?"

"Yes, and I think she's almost as excited as Ronnie," Carol said. "I never thought she'd be so enthusiastic about college."

"How's it working out for her and that young man?" Bennie asked. "Is he treating her right?"

"He seems to be," Carol admitted. "As far as I can tell, they're both settling right in to being married. I know I sure feel better about the whole thing than I did two months ago."

"That's good, that's real good," Bennie said. Carol had made no secret of her concern about Kim. "I know you're relieved."

"Very," Carol said. "In fact, the newlyweds are cooking me dinner tonight. I guess it's only fair—I've fed them supper for the last three Friday nights!"

Bennie and Carol both laughed, and Carol returned to her desk. Her day had been hectic, and she was already tense when Van called her at about two.

"How much did you have to pay for the Osso stock for Hugh Patton?" he asked cheerfully.

"Pay? The message I got was to sell a thousand shares," Carol said warily.

"What?" Van tended to become upset at the least little thing, and this was definitely no little thing. "What do you mean, you got a message to sell?"

"Just what I said," Carol replied tersely. "I found a message on my desk to sell."

Van swore sharply. "And you didn't—no, I should have—oh, hell, I dread having to tell Patton."

"Buy him some more Monday and I'll eat the difference," Carol said wearily, unwilling to argue about it. She checked the price of the stock and groaned inwardly. This was going to cost her a neat twelve hundred dollars. "Thanks a bunch."

"Likewise," Van said as he hung up.

Carol resisted the urge to bury her head in her hands. That was all she needed! She would just have to hustle that much harder next week to make up the difference. She took one of her stomach pills ahead of schedule and thoroughly chewed out the operator who had taken the garbled message. The operator was properly chastised, but the monetary loss was still Carol's. The stomach pill helped some, but she still felt a dull ache when Brandon came in her door around five.

"Still at it?" he asked. "I thought the market closed at three."

"It does," Carol said as she took her purse out of her drawer. "But there's usually enough paperwork to keep me here until five or six."

"Long day?" Brandon asked sympathetically. "You look awful," he added, blushing brightly when he realized what he had said. "Uh, I didn't mean—"

Carol looked at his face and burst out laughing. "Want some foot powder to brush your teeth with?" she teased before her face sobered. "No, I made a mistake that cost me a cool twelve hundred dollars this afternoon. I'm sure that took its toll on my looks."

Brandon whistled under his breath. "Yeah, it could have at that." He escorted Carol to the parking lot and opened the door to Kim's XR-7. "Kim said you wouldn't want to ride in the pickup since it doesn't have air conditioning."

"I wouldn't mind the truck one bit—from about October to April," Carol teased as Brandon backed out of the parking space. "But in August I appreciate the air conditioner."

With admirable skill Brandon contended with the clogged Katy Freeway.

"It's nice being driven for a change," Carol said as she leaned back and shut her eyes.

"I hope you don't mind that I asked Dad to come to dinner tonight too," Brandon said. "He's taken us out a couple of times, and I wanted to repay his hospitality."

Carol's eyes snapped open. "Not at all, that's great, Brandon," she said more calmly than she felt. She felt a blush creep up her face as she remembered her last encounter with Harlan Stone. She had done her best to forget that she had cried in his arms and shared a passionate kiss with him the night of Kim and Brandon's wedding. She had known she would have to see him again sooner or later, but that hadn't prevented her from dreading the occasion.

Carol stared out at the heat shimmering off the concrete and missed the speculative look Brandon cast her way. Actually, his father had invited himself to dinner when he had found out that Carol was going to be there, and Brandon wondered what his father was up to. His father and Kim's mother? They didn't have one thing in common.

Harlan's car was already parked in front of the apartment when Brandon pulled up beside it. Carol plastered a friendly smile on her face and followed Brandon up the stairs. Kim greeted her mother with a hug and a kiss. "Hi, Mom. I'm glad to see you tonight."

Carol ran a motherly eye over her daughter. "You're looking wonderful, Kim," she said, noting Kim's healthy tan and glowing eyes.

"I second that," Harlan said, looking from the rested, tanned daughter to her pale, tired-looking mother. Somebody ought to tell that woman not to work so hard, he thought.

Kim looked down at her burgeoning figure and made a face. "I'm starting to look like Buddha."

"Naw, his navel's different," Brandon teased as he placed a tender kiss on Kim's cheek. "Really, Kim, you look great."

"And if you didn't, he'd tell you," Carol teased, deliberately drawing another blush from Brandon. "He's already informed me I look awful," she said to Harlan, her eyes twinkling in her tired face.

"Tact was never one of his strong points," Harlan said. "Here, let's have a seat. You do look a little tired."

"But can't I do anything in the kitchen, Kim?" Carol protested.

"Brandon can help, Mom," Kim assured her. "Sit down and I'll bring you a little something to nibble on until the casserole's ready. Come on, Brandon, you get to be the assistant chef," she said as she grabbed Brandon's hand and disappeared into the kitchen.

Carol sank into the couch and kicked off her shoes. "I don't need to be invited twice," she said.

"Neither do I," Harlan said as he sat back down in the easy chair and sipped his glass of beer. "We've spent the last three days at a River Oaks mansion trimming trees they've let go for the last ten years. You wouldn't believe the mess those trees are in."

"That's a shame in a neighborhood like that," Carol said as she observed Harlan unobtrusively. Calm, relaxed, he seemed to have forgotten about their passionate encounter the night of the wedding, and Carol responded gratefully to his bland cordiality. She was laughing helplessly at his imitation of the cantankerous old widow at the River Oaks house when Kimberly brought in a plate of hors d'oeuvres and set it down on the coffee table.

"Here's a little something to hold us," she said as she sat down on the couch beside Carol. "The casserole will be a few more minutes, and Brandon's making the iced tea."

"These look interesting," Carol said as she sampled a cracker with spread on it. "Oh, this is good," she said as the mildly flavored cheese spread melted in her mouth.

Kim thanked her as Harlan picked up a cracker with a different spread on it. He popped it in his mouth and his eyes widened a little as he chewed it. "Delicious, but definitely on the spicy side," he said as he drank a little beer and reached for another. "Try one, Carol, they're great."

Carol eyed the crackers warily. "I'd love to, but I better not," she admitted.

"Stomach kicking up again?" Kim asked sympathetically.

"Oh, have you been sick?" Harlan asked, surprised. "I heard there was a virus going around."

"Nothing as dramatic as that, I'm afraid," Carol admitted. "I have an ulcer, and it's been bothering me today." She helped herself to one of the plain crackers.

Harlan managed to look surprised and sympathetic at the same time. "How did you end up with an ulcer? Middle-aged businessmen are supposed to get them."

"Anyone in a pressure-filled job can get one," Carol replied, "and I definitely have a stressful job."

"Mom's had the ulcer for almost three years," Kim said as she got up. "Be back in a minute."

"I didn't realize stockbroking was that stressful," Harlan said thoughtfully, his expression slightly disapproving.

"You thought we all sat in fancy offices and made a lot of money, right?" Carol teased. "No, we're basically salesmen, and we work on a commission. The more I sell, the more money I make." She made a face. "And when I foul up like I did today, I lose money. A cool twelve hundred this afternoon, to be exact. I'll have to hustle that much harder next week to make up for it."

Harlan glanced at Carol's face. No wonder she looked tired! "And your stomach's been hurting, right?" He frowned.

Carol nodded. "But that's just the price I have to pay for the successful career," she said, dismissing Harlan's obvious disapproval.

Harlan thought a minute. "I can't see any career being worth an ulcer," he said as he stroked his chin with his thumb. "I don't think I'd ever stick around if it did that to me."

"But what about your business? Doesn't it mean a lot to you?"

"Not all that much," Harlan admitted. "I enjoy it, and it's an income, but that's about all. It's never given me a stomachache."

Carol stared at Harlan thoughtfully. "I can't imagine not having a career that means a lot to me," she said slowly. She and Harlan stared into one another's eyes for a minute before she picked up another cracker and bit into it. She had known before that she and Harlan had different life-styles, of course, but it wasn't until this moment that Carol had realized just how different their outlooks were. Apparently his tree trimming business wasn't much more than a job to him, one that he did well and that put food on his table and a roof over his head, but that was all it was to him. Her career, on the other hand, provided her with her income and life-style as well as a good measure of her self-esteem. She cared passionately about her career, since in her eyes it made her a lot of what she was.

Harlan finished his beer and set his glass on a coaster. He too had realized with something of a jolt just how far apart his and Carol Venson's value systems were. Sure, he was glad he owned the business, but it wasn't everything to him, not by a long shot. But, apart from Kim, stockbroking seemed to be Carol Venson's whole life. Harlan felt a twinge of pity for her. If anything ever happened to her job with Purcell-Smith, she was going to be in a sorry state. He simply couldn't understand how anybody's career could mean that much to them.

Kim carried her casserole into the small dining area. "It's on the table," she said cheerfully. Brandon followed her in with a bowl of salad and a basket of rolls.

Harlan held Carol's chair for her. "Kim, this looks delicious," she said as Harlan sat down beside her.

Brandon held the chair for Kim. "She can really cook. Here, try the casserole," he said as he passed it to Carol.

The four of them passed all the dishes, and Kim's dinner proved to taste as good as it looked. Kim and Brandon related more tales about their honeymoon, and Carol asked casually how much Jack's check had been for.

Kim raised her eyebrows. "It was for a couple of hundred, but we didn't need it for our honeymoon after all. I haven't even cashed it yet."

"You ought to go ahead and cash it even if you don't need it right now," Carol said. "Put the money into your savings account."

"We could cash it and get a stereo," Brandon said. "That's the one thing we didn't get for a wedding present, and I miss having one."

"I'd rather put the money in the bank," Kim said quickly. "We might need it later."

Brandon shot Kim a dark look. "There's more than enough to pay your tuition and books next week, if that's what you're worried about," he said shortly. "We could buy the stereo and not go into debt for it."

"I don't want to get a stereo, Brandon," Kim said quietly.

Carol could tell that her daughter's temper was rising. "Why don't you two talk this over later?" she asked quickly. "Have you decided what courses you're going to take this fall, Kim?"

Temporarily distracted, Kim told them what courses she planned to sign up for, and they spent the rest of dinner talking about college in general and Kim's plans in particular. Brandon joined the discussion enthusiastically, and Carol felt that the young man was sincere in his support of Kim's education. She could also sense that, for some reason, college had become more important to Kim than it had been in the past, and perhaps that was why she wanted to put her father's money away rather than spend it. But Carol remembered all too well how a minor disagreement could turn major when neither party was willing to compromise, and she decided that she was going to say something to Kim tonight before she left, if she had a chance.

Kim produced an angel-food cake that she admitted was storebought but was still delicious. Harlan and Brandon helped Carol and Kim clear the table, and with Kim's blessing Harlan and Brandon disappeared into the bedroom to watch a preseason football game on television.

Carol carried the last of the dishes into the kitchen. "Do you want these in the dishwasher?" she asked.

"Here, I'll take those," Kim said. She deftly loaded the dishes and filled the dispenser with soap.

She was about to push the button when Carol put her fingers over the control knob. "Could we talk in here for a minute before you turn on the dishwasher?" Carol asked quietly.

"Sure," Kim said. "Is anything wrong?"

"Not yet, but if you're not careful, there could be," Carol said. Kim looked at her with puzzlement. "I'm talking about your dad's check."

"Oh. Well, I think we ought to save it in case I need it later for college. I might need it for books or something, you know."

"Yes, you might, but then again, you might not," Carol said. "But whether you do or you don't, is it worth fighting a major battle over it?"

"We didn't have a major battle," Kim protested.

"No, but if I know you and Brandon, it definitely has the possibility of becoming one when the topic comes up again. You were both only children and are used to having your own way. Now you have to share things for the first time in your life, and neither of you is used to doing that. If you both don't learn to compromise, you're going to have some hard times ahead. Believe me, Kim, that was a lot of what happened to your father and me. It was a toss-up sometimes which of us had a harder head."

"You mean I just let him take my money and spend it the way he wants to?" Kim asked indignantly.

"Kim," Carol said mildly, "the check was a gift to both of you, even if it was made out in your name. Besides, Brandon's paying your tuition and buying your books this fall, even though I was more than willing to, so it's not like he's being tight-fisted with you or trying to stand in your way. Talk about it some, and if it means that much to him, buy the stereo."

Kim thought a minute. "I guess you're right," she conceded.

"That's the key to making a marriage work, Kim. Learn to talk and to compromise a little. It will make all the difference."

"I will, Mom." Kim placed a gentle kiss on Carol's cheek and turned on the dishwasher.

Carol returned to the living room and looked around for her purse. "Did you see where I put my purse?" she asked her daughter. "I need one of my stomach pills."

"I put it in the bedroom," Kim said. "Want me to get it for you?"

"That's all right," Carol said. She walked down the short hall past the second small bedroom and was about to open the door when she heard the sound of masculine laughter coming from the room.

She paused, her hand on the doorknob, and listened as she heard Brandon's voice.

"Did Mom really do that? That's hilarious." They both laughed again.

Carol knew that she shouldn't be eavesdropping, but she was curious to hear what Harlan and his son were talking about.

"Yes, she did. But back to you and Kim. Remember, you're the man around here, and you have to act like it. Start out that way, and the rest of it will be a breeze."

At his words, Carol felt her anger flare, and it was all she could do to keep from marching in the room and giving them both a piece of her mind. And to think she had been telling Kim that she needed to compromise. If Brandon was foolish enough to take Harlan's advice, the marriage didn't have a chance, because Kim wasn't the kind of girl to put up with bullying from anyone.

Carol turned the knob and pushed the door open with a jerk. "Excuse me," she said shortly. "I need the medicine out of my purse." She shot Harlan a dirty look and carried her handbag out of the bedroom.

Carol and Kim visited until the game was over. She started to say something else to Kim, but decided that she had said enough, and there was always the chance that Brandon had the good sense to ignore his father's advice. Carol could barely force herself to be civil to Harlan when he and Brandon joined them in the living room, and Harlan was both baffled and put out with her by the end of the evening.

They both thanked Kim and Brandon again for dinner. "Kim, where did I lay my keys?" Brandon asked as he fished around in his pockets.

"I don't know," she said, poking her fingers between the cushions of the couch.

"Still losing your keys?" Harlan teased. "He loses one set a month."

"That's a pain," Carol murmured.

"Found them!" Kim said a moment later as she handed the keys to Brandon.

"Where are you going this late at night?" Harlan asked.

"He's taking me home," Carol said quickly. "My car is in the shop."

"Why don't I run you home and save Brandon a trip?" Harlan asked, thinking that on the way he could find out why Carol had turned so cold halfway through the evening. Maybe there was a reason Jack Venson had left her.

"Sure," Carol replied. She wasn't that thrilled about riding home with Harlan, but it would give her a perfect opportunity to express her anger.

"If you don't mind, Dad, I would appreciate it," Brandon said.

Carol and Harlan wished Brandon and Kim good night, and Carol followed Harlan down the stairs to his car.

"It isn't quite a Lincoln, but it will get you home," Harlan said as he opened the door for her.

"Monte Carlo's are nice cars. I drove one for five years," Carol said stiffly.

Harlan pulled out of the parking lot and lit them both a cigarette. "Would you care to tell me what happened to turn you into the north wind?" Harlan asked.

Carol didn't pretend that she didn't understand. "I don't appreciate having my daughter's marriage interfered with," she said coolly. "When I went to the bedroom to get my purse I heard you talking to Brandon. Those kids are going to have a hard enough time making that marriage work without a lot of bad advice on your part."

"I was interfering?" Harlan snapped. "I'm not the one who started spelling out conditions to Brandon before they had even gotten married! Besides, you were off in the kitchen talking to Kim, weren't you?" He braked suddenly for a light, throwing Carol forward.

"Yes, but I wasn't in there tonight filling her head with a bunch of outdated garbage," Carol said angrily. "You want to know what I was saying to Kim tonight? I told her to compromise. I was in there trying to tell my child to get along with yours, and you were in there telling yours to 'be a man' and walk all over mine! I don't appreciate that. Now, every time they have a disagreement, he's going to try to have his own way, only she's too hardheaded to let him, and—"

"Whoa!" Harlan exclaimed loudly. "Hold on there, lady."

Stunned, Carol could only stare at him in amazement. Harlan pulled over and parked under a tree. "Do I have your complete and undivided attention?" he asked quietly as he turned off the engine.

"You most certainly do!"

"Thank you. Now, I don't know what you thought you heard in there, but I was *not* telling my son to walk all over your daughter."

"You told him that he was a man, and that he needed to act like one," Carol said bitterly. "You told him that if he acted like a man from the beginning, the rest would take care of itself. Only it won't. She'll get fed up and leave him."

"Like you did?" Harlan asked.

"Yes."

"And how do you think a man—a real man—acts?" Harlan paused, then said softly, "A real man, not one like that jerk you were married to, always compromises with his wife. He's not afraid to let her have her way about something that's important to her. My dad used to remind me to act like a man when Wanda and I would argue, and I was reminding Brandon of the same thing tonight. I was telling him to compromise, the same as you were telling Kim."

"Oh." A hot blush crept up Carol's face as she realized how badly she had misjudged him. "Harlan, I'm sorry," she whispered, thoroughly contrite. "I had no idea what you meant when you told him to act like a man."

Harlan reached out and felt the heated blush on her cheeks. "That's all right, you didn't know what I was trying to tell him," he said quietly.

They rode in silence to Carol's house. Harlan parked in the driveway and glanced over at her embarrassed face. "I'm willing to accept a few kisses in apology," he said softly. He tipped Carol's face up and before she could object he met her lips in a tender caress.

The kiss started out gentle, an act of exploration as much as of passion. Carol's lips moved ever so slightly as she gently nibbled Harlan's lips and the lightly whiskered skin around it. His skin was a little salty and had a flavor that was uniquely his own, and Carol felt her hands sliding up and resting on his shoulders, caressing them with the tips of her fingers. Harlan nibbled the soft bow of Carol's mouth, teasing and exploring, but gradually, as the light caresses were no longer enough, they deepened the intensity of their embrace, sliding closer together on the front seat.

Harlan's lips grew more demanding, drawing from Carol a deep longing to share even greater intimacies with him. She plunged her fingers into the thick hair at his nape, and her tongue boldly invaded the warmth of his mouth, tangling with his in a sensual assault. Carol groaned as his arms crept around her and caressed the warmth of her back and shoulders. His arms were warm and inviting, a place of shelter as well as passion.

The blood pounded in his ears as Harlan stroked her nape with trembling fingers. She was so small and soft and inviting! He resisted the urge to push her down on the seat and cover her body with his, but his hands seemed to have a will of their own and one of them found the roundness of her breast through the smooth fabric of her blouse. He heard her sigh as she thrust herself closer, and his breath came in quick bursts as his fingers stroked her nipple, making it rise into a small bud of desire.

Sweet, sweet madness, Carol thought as she reveled in the pleasure of Harlan's touch. No man had ever set her on fire like he did. And she could sense that she was doing the same thing to him. Eagerly, she stroked his hard, lean muscles, feeling the strength in his chest and back. He groaned when she found one masculine nipple and teased it through the thin fabric of his shirt. His hands slid lower and his fingers circled her narrow waist.

"Dear God, you're tiny," he said as his lips caressed her cheek. "I can almost span your waist with my fingers."

Carol looked down at his hands linked possessively around her waist. "Your fingers are long," she said as she covered his hands with her own. She stared into his shadowed face. "Am I forgiven?"

"You were forgiven before I kissed you," Harlan said. "The kiss was to make you feel better. Did it?"

"It sure did," Carol admitted shyly. He had certainly taken her mind off her embarrassment!

"Carol, I wouldn't tell Brandon to do anything that would get that marriage in trouble," Harlan assured her. "I want it to succeed as much as you do."

"Thank you," Carol said as she leaned against him. "What do you suppose they'll do with the money?"

"I don't know, but I'm willing to bet they find a hundred-dollar stereo someplace and bank the rest." Harlan laughed. He got out and opened the door for Carol. "Your trees are a mess," he commented idly. "I'll come over tomorrow and do something about them."

"Oh, no, that's all right," Carol said quickly. "You don't have to worry about my trees."

"I've got to—everybody knows my son's married to your daughter, and these trees are a lousy advertisement for Stone's Tree Service," Harlan said firmly as he swooped down and kissed Carol again. Carol gave herself up to passion, and by the time Harlan finally pulled away and left she had completely forgotten about her trees.

Carol took a long shower before she put on her nightgown and climbed into bed. She shivered a little as she relived the passionate kisses she and Harlan had shared, and her expression was wistful as she turned out the light. Harlan had drawn a passionate response from her she didn't even know she was capable of. It was a shame that physical attraction was all they had in common, she thought as she closed her eyes.

What was that buzzing sound? Carol wondered as she turned over and buried her head under the pillow. She had not set her alarm last night, since today was Saturday, and she hoped whatever was buzzing would stop so she could go back to sleep. She had managed to muffle the sound with the pillow and was drifting back to sleep when she heard the sound of something large and heavy thudding down onto her roof.

"What in God's name?" she cried as she jumped out of bed and ran out to the patio off her bedroom. She skidded to a halt when she encountered the huge cherry picker parked in the middle of her backyard.

Harlan was seated in the basket aiming a chain saw at a low-hanging branch. He looked down when the door flew open and stared at Carol. The sun shone brightly through her sheer gown, affording him a look at all of her feminine attributes. Her body shone through, shapely and supple, and her tousled hair and sleepy expression only added to her appeal. His throat grew dry and he was glad that the basket hid the evidence of his arousal that was all too obvious in his tight jeans.

"I—I forgot you were coming," Carol said as she backed into the house and shut the door behind her. She hastily grabbed her robe and wrapped it around her. Another branch hit the roof as she stepped back out on the patio.

Harlan switched off the chain saw. "Mornin'," he said, hoping he sounded calmer than he felt. "Sorry if I woke you."

"That's all right," Carol said. "Give me a half hour, and I'll have coffee on."

Harlan grinned. "Thanks," he said as he turned the saw back on.

Thoroughly flustered, Carol brushed her hair and dressed in culottes and a matching blouse. She was just spooning coffee into the coffeemaker when Harlan knocked on the back door. From the various thuds on her roof Carol gathered that he had been working hard on the trees, and the light film of perspiration on his face confirmed it.

"It's going to be a scorcher out there today," he said as he sat down at the kitchen table.

"How about iced tea instead of hot coffee?"

Harlan nodded and she dumped the coffee back into the can. "Have you had breakfast?" she asked.

"No, since Brandon's gone I've started skipping it," Harlan admitted.

"Shame on you," Carol scolded lightly. She warmed two sweetrolls in the microwave and sat down across from Harlan. This close, she could smell his aftershave and the faint odor of his perspiration, and she felt a ridiculous urge to sit in his lap and pick up where they had left off the night before. How could a man who was so wrong for her be so attractive?

"Brandon will be over later," Harlan volunteered as he swallowed a bite of sweetroll. "I asked him to come early, but he wasn't too thrilled about that idea."

"I can understand that," Carol murmured. A blush crept up her face. She had been a newlywed once, and she could understand all too well why Brandon didn't want to get up early!

"It's hard thinking of them as adults, isn't it?" Harlan asked softly.

"It sure is," Carol admitted. "I think all parents feel that way about their children's sexuality."

They finished breakfast in a companionable silence, and Harlan returned to his work while Carol called the car dealer. The company sent someone to pick her up, and Carol spent most of the day running errands and grocery shopping.

It was after four when she pulled into her driveway. Brandon's truck was parked in front of the house, and the cherry picker was now in the front yard. Both men were grubby, and Harlan had removed his sweat-soaked shirt and thrown it on the sidewalk. Carol could not stop herself from staring at his broad chest as he picked up a branch and heaved it off the roof. Rivulets of sweat streaked the thick dark hair that tangled its way down to his belt. Tearing her eyes away from his chest, she met his friendly gaze with a smile of her own. "You still at it?"

"We're just cleaning up," Brandon said as he stacked the branches in the back of his truck. "We left the best of the wood for firewood."

"Thanks." Carol looked up at her beautifully manicured trees. "I didn't know this yard could look so good!" she marveled. "You've done a great job."

"Thanks," Harlan said.

"Come on in for iced tea when you're finished," Carol said as she carried her groceries inside.

They appeared at the back door a few minutes later. "You must be burning up," Carol said as she handed a glass of iced tea to each of them. Harlan had pulled on a clean T-shirt he must have had with him, but they were both still hot and sweaty. Carol felt a new respect for them—they worked like this every day!

"I needed that," Brandon said as he drained the glass and poured himself another from the pitcher on the counter.

"Pass that pitcher over here," Harlan said.

They drank three glasses of tea each. Carol put their empty glasses in the dishwasher and took her checkbook from her purse. "How much do I owe you?" she asked quietly.

Harlan and Brandon both looked at her with surprise.

"Nothing," Harlan said.

"But—"

"Carol, you're family," Brandon said, as though that explained everything.

Carol looked from Harlan to Brandon and slowly slipped her checkbook back into her purse. "You don't know how much I appreciate this," she said gratefully. "Is there anything I can do to thank you both?"

"You can feed me dinner again next week," Brandon said hopefully.

"You're on," Carol said. "What about you, Harlan?"

"You can take me out to eat sometime," Harlan said. "Without the kids." He winked, and Brandon made a face at him.

"Sounds great," Carol said. She was a little amused by Harlan's condition, but grateful for the work he had put in today. "How about this evening? Do you have plans?"

"No," Harlan said. "Is seven too early?"

"Seven's fine. And since it's your evening, do you want to go someplace casual, or do you want to go all out?"

"Since you're paying, let's go all out." Harlan laughed. "See you in a little while."

Carol was ready thirty minutes early.

CHAPTER FIVE

Carol was waiting eagerly when Harlan rang the doorbell. "Quite a transformation," she said approvingly as he stood before her in an expensive sport coat, his hair still damp from the shower. "Come in. Would you like a drink?"

"I'd love one," Harlan said. He made himself comfortable in the family room while she mixed him a Scotch and soda and herself a weaker one.

"Can you have that?" he asked as she handed him his drink and sat down beside him.

"I'm not supposed to, but I bend the rules a little sometimes," Carol admitted. "After you and Brandon left, I went out and took another look at the trees. I still can't believe they look so good."

"It was our pleasure," Harlan said. He shifted his shoulder and winced.

"Did you hurt yourself today?"

"No, that shoulder's been stiff for three or four months now," Harlan said. "I guess it's just age."

Carol made a face. "Don't say that, I'm just a little behind you. How old are you, anyway?"

"Nosy," Harlan teased, bringing a blush to Carol's cheeks. "As a matter of fact, I'm forty."

"Ancient," Carol murmured. "If you'll sit in that chair over there, where I can reach you, I'll see what I can do to take the soreness out of your shoulder." Even if he hadn't hurt himself today working on her trees, he couldn't have done his shoulder much good. "Take off your jacket."

Harlan looked amused, but he followed her directions. He winced when Carol's fingers dug into the tight muscles surrounding the sore joint, but her painful touch soon turned to pleasure, and he could feel her taking the tightness from the muscles and joint. Carol fought to keep her touch firm and impersonal. The strength of his shoulders and arm were doing crazy things to her pulse rate, and she longed to run her hands down the hollow of his spine and caress his narrow waist. She kneaded his muscles until she could feel them relax under her fingers. "Better?" she asked.

"Much," Harlan said gratefully. He finished the rest of his drink. "Ready to go?"

Carol nodded and locked the door as they left the house. Harlan opened the car door for her.

"Where to?" he asked as he started the engine.

"What would you like?" Carol asked. "Something old and very elegant, or someplace new and trendy?"

"Old and elegant, please," Harlan said.

Carol suggested a French restaurant in the River Oaks area. They chatted amiably as Harlan made his way across town and pulled up in front of the restaurant.

"I've never been here," he said. "Am I underdressed?"

"Oh, darn, I forgot," Carol said. "Nothing less than a dinner jacket and white gloves for you and a formal for me."

Harlan looked over and saw that her eyes were twinkling.

"You look good enough to walk in any restaurant in Houston," she assured him.

He grinned. As he got out and then opened her door and took her arm, Carol thought that although Harlan might have a blue-collar job and only a high school diploma, his manners would have put those of many professional men to shame. Heads turned as they entered the restaurant, and as they passed a large smoked mirror Carol was astonished at what a handsome couple they made. The headwaiter seated Carol and handed them both a menu printed in French.

"You're going to have to help me out with this thing," Harlan admitted after one look.

"Let's see, the third entree on the left is a delicious veal dish. I've had that a couple of times. And any of the fish or poultry dishes on the right are good too. The waiter will be able to help us both when he gets here."

Harlan glanced over the top of his menu. "Don't speak it either, huh?"

"No. I don't even speak Spanish, and in my work it would be extremely useful if I did. A lot of Mexican businessmen like to invest their money in the States."

Their waiter came and assisted them in choosing main dishes. Since Carol had enjoyed the veal before, she chose that, and Harlan ordered one of the fish dishes.

"Do you speak Spanish?" Carol asked as the waiter departed.

"Enough to tell the few Mexicans who work for me what to do. They're all legal, but some of them haven't been here too long."

"I want to go to night school and learn enough Spanish to work with Mexican investors," Carol said. "And I will, if I ever get the time. I thought I'd have more time now that Kim's gone, but it hasn't worked out that way. It seems like the more I do, the more I have to do, at least where my job's concerned."

"How many hours a week do you put in?" Harlan asked.

"Officially or unofficially?" Carol asked. The waiter put their bowls of onion soup in front of them and Carol tasted hers.

"Total hours," Harlan said.

Carol thought a minute. "Fifty-five or sixty, most weeks," she said. "Part of it depends on what the market is doing."

Harlan whistled under his breath. "Those are long hours," he said a little disapprovingly.

"Yes, but I don't put in my hours out in the hot sun," Carol reminded him. "And I can do some of it, the letter writing and reading, for example, when I choose to." She paused while she took another spoonful of soup. "But don't you have paperwork too, if you own the business?"

Harlan made a face. "Don't I! I have to spend a couple of afternoons a week doing it." He leaned toward her. "Don't tell anyone, but I'd much rather be out in the hot sun that cooped up shuffling papers!"

Carol laughed. "Ever thought of expanding your business?" she asked.

"Sure, I think about it at least once a week, but that's all I'm ever going to do about it," Harlan said.

"Why?" Carol asked, curious. Adding more clients was what stockbroking was all about, and she strove constantly to increase her list of customers.

"Because I have enough business and enough money," Harlan said simply. He smiled when Carol looked puzzled. "Carol, I earn a nice living and don't have to kill myself doing it. I don't want or need any more than that."

"But what about the excitement of expanding?" Carol asked. "Aren't you interested in doing it for the challenge, even if you don't need the money?"

"Not at all," Harlan answered. "I put in forty to fifty hours a week, more in the summer than in the winter, and in that time I earn enough to live comfortably, and I could have educated Brandon if he had wanted it. After that my time's my own, and I'm free to enjoy fishing or boating or just sitting around doing nothing. If I expanded the business, I'd have to give up some of that free time, and I don't want to do that."

"Oh."

Harlan reached over and patted her hand. "I have no burning desire to set the world on fire, and I know that's hard for an ambitious person like you to understand. I think I'm what's known as a Type B personality."

Carol smiled faintly. "I guess that makes me an A plus," she admitted. "You're right. I do have trouble understanding someone like you. Success in business is very important to me."

"Why is it so important to you?" Harlan asked. "Have you always been so determined to be a success?"

"In a way, but not in the business world, and it certainly didn't used to matter this much," Carol admitted. "I guess I'm still trying to compensate for messing up so badly when I was younger."

"Your divorce bothered you that much?" Harlan asked.

"That was just part of it," Carol admitted. "When I had to get married, a pregnant bride was still considered a failure. I had to abandon the education that I wanted very badly, and then the marriage turned out to be a complete dud. My self-image took a lot of blows in those years. I guess I'm still trying to make up for all that failure by being the best damned stock-broker at Purcell-Smith." She smiled faintly. "And I just might make it."

"I can understand that," Harlan said quietly. "But aren't you being a little hard on yourself? You may have gotten pregnant before you were married, but you've been a wonderful mother to your daughter, and it seems to me that your ex can take as much credit for the failed marriage as you. On second thought, I've met the man. I don't think you should blame yourself at all!"

Carol smiled warmly at him. "Thanks," she said softly.

The waiter brought their dishes and they ate their dinner slowly, savoring every bite of the delicately flavored food. Over dinner, Carol told Harlan about some of the amusing things that had happened to her as a stockbroker and about some of the really good strokes of intuition that had served her well. Harlan in turn told her about some of the funny things that had happened while he was trimming trees and how he decided which limbs to cut and how much to remove. Carol soon came to the conclusion that trimming trees well was a form of art.

They lingered over coffee, and Harlan suggested a late movie. Carol agreed, wondering what kind of movie would appeal to Harlan, and was pleasantly surprised to find herself enjoying Meryl Streep's latest picture.

"That was delightful," she said as they walked back to Harlan's car. "Her acting has such class."

"She has class," Harlan said almost dreamily.

Carol glanced up and saw an almost smitten expression on his face. "Got a crush on her, Harlan?" she teased gently.

Harlan blushed in the light of a street lamp. "I could do a lot worse," he said. "Besides, she always does really fine films."

"You don't have to defend your preference to me," Carol said mildly, a little chagrined with herself for being surprised at Harlan's taste in movie stars.

Both loathe to end the evening, they stopped at an all-night restaurant for dessert. They talked about movies, both recent and old, and stayed long after their apple pie was gone. Finally, Harlan drove her home and parked in her driveway. "I don't know when I've enjoyed an evening more," Harlan said.

"I had a wonderful time."

"Have you made plans for next weekend already?" Harlan asked.

"Uh, no," Carol said, caught off-guard by the question.

"Great. How about next Friday night, then?" Harlan asked. "About the same time?"

"I don't think so, Harlan," Carol said slowly.

Harlan's smiled faded from his face. "I thought you said you weren't busy," he said.

Carol bit her lip. "I'm not," she said. "I just don't think we should start seeing each other, that's all."

"Why not?" he demanded, sliding across the seat toward her and grasping her arm in fingers that were gentle but firm.

"Why do you want to go out with me again?" Carol parried nervously. "We don't have anything in common except Brandon and Kim. We're very different, you know."

"Don't you think that's what it takes to keep a relationship interesting?" Harlan countered smoothly. "I'd like to go out with you again because I'm attracted to you. I've been attracted to you since the first day we met, and unless I'm a complete moron, you're also attracted to me. I think we could have something very special between us, Carol."

"But we don't have anything in common," Carol protested weakly.

"You mean I'm a tree trimmer and you're a stockbroker," Harlan jeered. "You don't want to go out with me because you're a snob."

"That's not true!" Carol said, trying to wrench her arm away from Harlan's hand.

"Oh, but I think it is," he said smoothly. "You don't want to go out with me because I'm not a member of your socioeconomic circle."

"I am not the snob you keep telling me I am!" Carol snapped.

"All right, prove it," Harlan said as he tipped her face up to his. "Go out with me next weekend, and the weekend after that, and the one after that."

Carol tried to shake her head, but Harlan's lips came down on hers and she was again under his sensual spell. His kiss seduced her, controlled her, persuaded her as words could never have done that she wanted to see him again. When he sought entrance to her mouth she gave it willingly, opening herself to Harlan's sensual onslaught, letting the tide of passion sweep her away. She kissed him back, matching him kiss for kiss and caress for caress. His fingers boldly found and touched the tips of her breasts through the thin knit of the dress she wore, and Carol slipped her hands under Harlan's jacket, stroking his chest and moving around to his back.

Harlan groaned and pulled her even closer. He could feel her nipples straining against his broad chest, and desire curled in his midsection. He realized as well as Carol did that they didn't have much in common, that a relationship with her was bound to contain a number of land mines, but he didn't care. He wanted her, and he wanted her to come to him with no reservations. Harlan feathered gentle kisses over her face and neck, stopping at the scooped neck of her knit dress. He started to unbutton the dress, but remembered where they were and made do with caressing Carol's soft back and chest with his hands. Harlan finally pulled away from her, grinning wickedly at her as he straightened his shirt in the darkness. "I'll pick you up next Friday at seven," he said.

"But—"

"No buts. You and I are going out next weekend," he said calmly as he walked Carol to her door. He kissed her again, long and lingeringly, his fingers playing up and down her spine until Carol thought she would scream with frustration. "See you next week."

Carol was too stunned to even protest as Harlan left her and drove away.

"Oh, wonderful," she said as she went inside. She and Harlan had no business seeing one another regularly. Not only were they in very different professions, but their outlook on life was totally at odds, and sooner or later that would cause them some major problems. But she knew now, after the way she had kissed Harlan just a couple of minutes ago, that he wouldn't let her back out of their date the next weekend. She was committed to spending another evening with Harlan Stone.

"Have any plans for the weekend?" Perry Simons asked as he stuck his head around the door. "Some of us are going out after work and thought you might like to come with us."

"Oh, thanks, Perry," Carol said, "but I'm busy this evening." Perry and his friends were very nice, and if she wasn't already busy, she would have been happy to go with them.

Perry wiggled his eyebrows up and down. "Hot date?" he teased.

Carol blushed. "He's just a friend," she said. "But thanks for thinking of me. Maybe next time, okay?"

"Okay," Perry replied. He shut the door behind him and Carol smiled to herself a little sheepishly. Harlan was some friend. But in the last week she had become used to the idea of spending another evening with him, and this morning she had found herself looking forward to it. She had thought of tracking him down and asking him where they were going, but she decided that was going too far and planned to wear a simple skirt and blouse that could take her anywhere.

Carol checked her watch and made a face. It was after two, and Rupert Martinez was supposed to come by before one with a check for the stock he wanted her to buy that afternoon. Mr. Martinez was one of Houston's most successful restaurateurs, and his account would be a feather in any stockbroker's cap. But if he didn't get there soon with his check, she wasn't going to be able to buy the stock that afternoon.

Carol flipped through her Rolodex and dialed Mr. Martinez's number. A receptionist answered the telephone and tried to put her off, but Carol was an expert at handling receptionists and soon her call was put through.

"Hello, Mr. Martinez, this is Carol Venson. Are you going to be able to get your check over here before the exchange closes?"

There was a moment of silence on the other end of the line. "Uh, Mrs. Venson, I do appreciate all the time you've spent with me in the last few weeks. But I had my nephew, who's a stockbroker too, buy the stock for me this morning."

Carol was stunned. "You what?"

"I had my nephew buy the stock for me." Mr. Martinez sounded a little embarrassed. "I appreciate all the tips, but I felt like I owed it to the boy to help him get started."

Carol's disbelief quickly turned to anger. "You mean that you took my tips and went to another stockbroker with them?" she asked coldly.

"Yes, I did," he said calmly.

"I don't imagine that you care, but what you did is highly unethical," Carol said angrily. "I hope you run your business with more integrity than you've exhibited in your dealings with me. Good day, Mr. Martinez." Carol slammed down the telephone and put her head in her hands. She had spent hours looking for just the right investments to lure Mr. Martinez onto her list, and he had probably intended all along to invest with his nephew.

"Damn!" she said aloud. Harold Rhodes was going to have a fit when he heard about this fish getting away.

She lit a cigarette and listened to the squawk box, but all she could think about was losing Rupert Martinez. To think he had the nerve to let his nephew buy the stocks she had recommended! She had wasted valuable time on this one, and after working so hard that week to make up for the money she had lost last Friday, the setback seemed intensified.

Carol made a few more phone calls and took care of some correspondence, but try as she might she could not dismiss Rupert Martinez's treachery, and the long wait in the heavy afternoon traffic did little to take her mind off her troubles. She started to call Harlan and cancel their date, but knowing him he would be on her doorstep demanding an explanation, and she wasn't up to giving one. Wearily, she showered and dressed, and was putting the finishing touches to her makeup when the doorbell rang.

Harlan smiled as she opened the door. "Hi. Could I hit you up for another drink tonight?" he asked pleasantly.

"Sure." Carol hoped her smile was natural as she led Harlan into the family room and fixed him a drink. The last thing she was in the mood for was a date, but she didn't want to be rude.

Carol took a stomach pill and didn't add any Scotch to her soda.

"Stomach bothering you again?" Harlan asked as she sat down beside him.

"A little," Carol admitted. "How was your week?"

"Long and hot," Harlan said. He launched into a story that under other circumstances Carol would have found funny, but that night she could barely keep her mind on what he was saying. She kept thinking about all the time she had wasted on Rupert Martinez, and the thoughts made her stomach twist with anger.

Harlan finished his drink and stood up. "One of my friends told me about a great new hamburger place in Westheimer," he said. "Is that all right with you?"

"Fine," Carol said distractedly. She followed Harlan out to his car and tried to make her share of the small talk on the way to the restaurant, but she was plainly distracted and Harlan shot her several looks on the way to the brightly lit restaurant.

"It's not quite the fancy place you took me last week, but it's supposed to be good," Harlan said as he opened Carol's car door.

"I'm sure it will be fine," she murmured as she walked past him and climbed the steps to the front door.

A young waiter escorted them to a table. Carol picked up her menu and opened it, but her eyes stared at the words unseeingly.

She really doesn't want to be here, Harlan thought angrily as disappointment shot through him. She looked miserable, and if her distracted expression was anything to go by, she could hardly wait for the evening to end. Maybe he shouldn't have been so quick to assume that she was interested in him—maybe last weekend she was just being gracious. Well, if that was the way she felt, he wouldn't force her to spend an entire evening in his company.

Harlan reached over and pushed Carol's menu down. "It's all right, I'll take you home," he said gruffly.

"What?"

"I said it's all right. I didn't think you really meant it, but if going out with me is making you this miserable, then I'll take you home. No hard feelings," Harlan explained.

"Oh, no!" Carol said quickly. "I'll admit that I'm miserable this evening, but it has nothing to do with you. Actually, this morning I was looking forward to our date. I'm sorry I'm such a lousy companion tonight."

Harlan's face cleared. "I thought you were miserable because I more or less twisted your arm into coming."

"No, that wasn't it."

"Well, what happened to make you so unhappy?" Harlan asked. "Your job again?"

Carol nodded. "Let's order and I'll tell you about it."

Harlan signaled the waiter and they both ordered hamburgers with the works, although Carol doubted that she would be able to eat much of hers.

"Now, tell me what happened to upset you," Harlan said.

"I worked all week looking for the best possible investments for a man named Rupert Martinez," she said quietly. "He would have been a fantastic addition to my client list. I spent hours trying to help him. And then this afternoon he had the gall to tell me that he had his nephew, who just happens to be a stockbroker, buy him the stocks I had told him about. Looking back, I seriously doubt he ever intended to use my services—I think he was just stringing me along all the time."

"I hope you gave him a piece of your mind," Harlan said quietly.

"I did, but that isn't going to change anything. He still took my tips and went to someone else with them."

"That's unethical, I'll admit," Harlan said slowly. "But that kind of thing happens in business all the time. People cutting each other's throat, trying to cheat each other. Hasn't it happened to you before?"

"Sure, it has."

"And does it upset you this badly every time?" he asked quietly.

"Of course it does," Carol said. "It makes me furious!"

Harlan opened a package of crackers. "It sounds to me like you don't belong in stockbroking if you can't let something like this roll off your back."

Carol looked up at him angrily. "What am I supposed to do, give up a well-paying and satisfying job just because it upsets me sometimes?" she flared.

"This is the second Friday in a row you've left there tired and upset," Harlan said calmly. "Do you ever leave work in a good mood?"

"Of course!" she retorted, unwilling to admit that she left work in a rotten mood more often than not. "Look, Harlan, I know you don't understand, but I find the monetary and psychological rewards more than enough to outweigh the unpleasantness. So will you lay off my job?"

"I wasn't aware I'd laid into it," Harlan said, only the glitter in his eye betraying his anger.

"Oh, Harlan, you're right. I'm overreacting. But can't we agree to disagree about my job?" Carol asked.

"If you like," he said. He picked up a napkin and unfolded it, but stopped when he spotted an insignia in the corner. "Would you like to have a little revenge on Rupert Martinez?" he asked as he showed her the stamp. It appeared they were sitting in one of Rupert Martinez's restaurants.

Carol smiled wickedly. "You bet!"

Harlan signaled the waiter. "May I have our check, please?"

"But you haven't eaten, and your burgers are on the way!" the dumbfounded waiter protested.

He tried to argue, but Harlan insisted. Harlan handed the check to Carol, and as the waiter set their dishes in front of them she wrote across the check: We've decided to eat with my nephew, and signed her name.

"Will you be sure that Mr. Martinez gets this?" she asked sweetly as she handed the check to the waiter.

Harlan left a tip for the confused waiter, and Carol was shaking with laughter by the time they got into the car. "You're wicked!" she cried as she collapsed into the front seat.

"I wasn't going to spend my hard-earned money there after the way he treated you." Harlan looked at the restaurant wistfully. "Those burgers sure smelled good, though."

The next hamburger place they found didn't belong to Rupert Martinez, and the burgers were every bit as good as the first ones would have been. Relaxed and feeling a bit avenged, Carol ate her hamburger and fries, and even stole a few of Harlan's onion rings from his plate. Harlan was glad that she had relaxed enough to enjoy their evening together, but he simply couldn't understand why she insisted on staying with a job that left her worn out and miserable. She had the same deep circles under her eyes that night that she had last Friday, and

Harlan feared that before much longer they were going to be a permanent part of her face. Surely a bright woman like her could find another job, one that wouldn't wear her out before her time.

Carol finished the last of her snitched onion rings as Harlan signaled for the check.

"I guess I'll pay this one," he said wryly. He put his arm around her shoulders as they left the restaurant, and tipped her face up for a quick kiss before he opened the car door. "Wonderful—you taste just as oniony as I do," he teased as he unlocked the door.

"Thanks," Carol said dryly.

"It's not too late for a movie," Harlan said as he handed her the weekend section of the newspaper. "What would you like to see?"

Harlan turned on the overhead light and they huddled together over the movie ads. "How about this one?" Carol asked as she pointed to a rather heavy foreign film.

"If you like," Harlan said doubtfully.

"But I thought you'd like it," Carol said. "You said you like highbrow movies."

Harlan raised his eyebrow. "Did I say I was above occasional junk?"

"Well, in that case!" Carol pointed to a slapstick comedy she had heard about. Harlan grinned and kissed her on the nose as he turned on the ignition.

The movie was mindless and silly, and Carol loved every minute. At first she would sneak the occasional glance at Harlan to see how he was taking the nonsense, but after a while she didn't care what he thought; she was enjoying the movie too much. It was perfect therapy for the week she had just put in, and she found herself almost disappointed when the credits rolled and the lights came back on.

Harlan blinked in the light as he stood up. "Did you enjoy the movie?" he asked indulgently.

"I loved it," Carol exclaimed. "Did you enjoy it at all?"

"Of course I did." Harlan laughed. "But mostly I enjoyed watching this high-powered stockbroker laugh herself silly. Did you know that your giggle soars above everyone else's laugh?"

Carol blushed and had to admit that she didn't know. Harlan drove Carol home and parked in the driveway.

"Would you like to come in for a nightcap?" she asked softly, her tone indicating that the only thing she was offering him that night was a drink.

"Sure." He followed her inside and waited while she mixed him a drink and poured herself another club soda before sitting beside him on the couch.

"I enjoyed tonight," Harlan said as he reached out and stroked her nape.

"So did I," Carol admitted.

"Good grief, woman, you're still as wound up as a spring," Harlan said as he felt the tense muscles in her shoulders. "What am I going to do with you?" He took her drink from her and set it on the coffee table, then knelt by the side of the couch. "Lie down on your stomach and I'll rub your shoulders."

"No, Harlan, that's—" Carol started to protest, but he gently pushed her down on the couch.

"Now turn over," he said. "You rubbed my shoulder last week, so the least I can do is return the favor."

Obediently Carol flipped over and let Harlan work his magic on her back. At first his touch was firm and almost painful, but as Carol started to relax his fingers became pleasurable as they eased away the tension of the day. Carol shut her eyes and let herself flow with the unique sensations he was bringing to her. She felt herself unwinding for the first time all week as he ran his fingers through her hair, gently but firmly kneading her scalp until she was relaxed there too, and when he was satisfied his hands made their way down her neck to her back, where he massaged his way down to her waist. His touch was firm yet sensual, and Carol could feel desire start to unfurl deep within her.

As he patiently rubbed and squeezed the kinks out of her

muscles, desire put a fine mist of perspiration on Harlan's upper lip. He couldn't understand it. He wanted this fragile, thin, tired-looking woman as he had wanted no other in a very long time. Gradually, he let his hands drift below her waist as his fingers curled around her body. "Turn over," he whispered hoarsely.

Carol turned and Harlan loomed over her. She reached up to hold him, her lips meeting his in a joyous reunion. For long moments they kissed, their lips becoming reacquainted after a week's absence. Harlan eased himself up on the edge of the wide sofa and Carol moved over to give him more room. He put one arm under her head and lifted her slightly.

"You feel wonderful in my arms," he murmured as he stroked her waist with tender fingers.

"I like being in your arms," Carol admitted as she ran her hands over his strong chest. She could feel his heart beating and could see a pulse pounding in his throat. She reached up and covered the pulse with her thumb. "Do you like it when I touch you?"

Harlan nodded, kissing the inner curve of her arm. She caressed his face, and they melted into another passionate embrace, their lips mingling in a sensual sharing. He trailed kisses down her neck and onto her partly exposed shoulders, and Carol made no protest when he unbuttoned the first few buttons and pushed aside her blouse. He caressed her creamy shoulder with his lips and tongue before he grew bolder, grazing her breast near the edge of her bra. Then he undid a few more buttons and lowered her bra, pushing the straps off her shoulders.

"Beautiful, just beautiful," he said as he gazed at Carol's rosy-tipped breasts.

Carol waited, unconsciously holding her breath, as Harlan dipped his head and sampled first one breast and then the other. Carol could feel the desire curling through her entire body, and she whimpered with pleasure as Harlan continued to torment her. Eager to touch him the way he was touching her, she unbuttoned his shirt and pulled it from his slacks, running her fingers through the thick dark hair on his chest.

"I wanted to do this last Saturday," she admitted. "When I saw you with your shirt off."

"You would have shocked Brandon." Harlan laughed, her fingers sending shivers of pleasure through his body. He bent his head and continued to caress her breasts until she was shaking in his arms. "Are you ready for me?" he whispered as he looked into Carol's eyes.

She stared at him, reality piercing the sensual haze that had enveloped them both. Was she ready for him? Was she ready to commit herself to being this man's lover? She paused a moment and then she shook her head. "Oh, Harlan, I don't think so," she said miserably as she sat up.

"What do you mean, Carol?" Harlan asked incredulously.

Carol tugged her bra up over her breasts. "I'm not ready for that," she said softly.

"You mean not with me," Harlan said angrily. "Why must you deny what we have between us, Carol?"

"I'm not denying anything," Carol said. "And I mean not *even* with you. Believe me, Harlan, if I didn't take making love so seriously, I'd be with you tonight."

"Were you this particular with Jack Venson?" Harlan asked nastily. "Or with that fancy lawyer of yours? Or are you this particular only with tree trimmers?"

Carol recoiled as though she had been slapped. "I don't think that deserves an answer," she said stiffly. "Good night."

Harlan jerked on his shirt and buttoned it. "All right, that was below the belt and I'm sorry," he said gruffly. "But I wanted you tonight, and God forgive me if I thought you wanted the same thing." He marched to the door. "We'll do it your way for a while, Carol. But I swear, sooner or later you're going to be mine." He slammed the door behind him, and Carol heard his car roar out of the driveway.

Carol pulled her blouse together and leaned back into the cushions. He was right, and she knew it. Sooner or later, unless she pulled out of their relationship right now, she was going to give in to what they both wanted and become his lover.

Carol lit a cigarette and sat back to think. She was undeniably drawn to Harlan, and he to her. But weren't they just asking for a rocky relationship? Tonight was an excellent example. Although Harlan had been lovely to her, she knew that he didn't understand why she stayed with her job, and Carol didn't doubt that, under similar circumstances, Harlan would have quit. Sooner or later that kind of difference in values was bound to cause problems. But in spite of their differences, Carol doubted she had the strength to reject the relationship that Harlan offered her, and if she were honest with herself, she wasn't sure she really wanted to.

CHAPTER SIX

Carol pulled into the driveway and hopped out of the car. She had spent more time than usual that afternoon in the traffic, and Harlan was due in a half hour to take her and Kim and Brandon out to dinner. She fumbled with her keys and swore when she dropped them, but before long she was standing under a warm shower soaping her hair. She hummed under her breath as she worked in the fresh-smelling shampoo. For once she had left work in a good mood, and she was sincerely looking forward to an evening with Harlan and the kids.

Carol washed herself and rinsed quickly, pulling a thick, fluffy towel from the rack to dry herself. Pausing a moment, she stared at her reflection in the mirror, her nude body pink and glowing. Not perfect, but not bad for nearly forty. She reached down and touched one of the light, silvery marks that were the only outward evidence that she had borne Kim. Jack had poked fun at the marks the entire time they were married, and Carol wondered if Harlan was the kind of man to tease her about them. She had spent the last month holding Harlan off physically, but if they continued to see one another, it wasn't going to be much longer before they were lovers, and Carol wondered if her body would please him.

Shrugging, Carol put on lacy panties and a matching bra. She and Harlan had been seeing one another regularly lately, but she hadn't been willing to become his lover, and she had to admit that to an extent she had been holding him off emotionally as well. She knew Harlan was ready for a deeper relationship with her, and he was finding her position frustrating, but Carol was very unsure that putting their relationship on a more intimate level would be wise. She had found Harlan a marvelous companion, witty and warm and funny, and she had been surprised at just how much they did have in common. They both loved a good movie, serious or silly, it didn't matter, and she was surprised and delighted to discover that Harlan loved haunting museums as much as she did. As a girl Carol had loved to dance, and Harlan had reawakened this love in her one night when he drove her to Pasadena and took her to Gilley's, where they listened to western music and danced every dance until closing time. And of course they had Kim and Brandon in common. They were both relieved that the young couple's marriage seemed to be working out, and they were both looking forward eagerly to the birth of their grandchild.

But they had a lot of differences too, Carol had to admit as she pulled her dress over her head. They had never come out and discussed their opposing outlooks on life since their first date, but Carol could tell by little things that Harlan didn't and probably couldn't understand just how important her career was to her. He had come by her office one day at noon to take her out to lunch, and had been surprised and disappointed to learn that she never left the speaker during market hours for more than a few minutes. He had been a good sport and had brought in a pizza to share at her desk, but she could tell he didn't understand why she wouldn't play hooky just that once. And one day Carol went by his office on her way home from work only to learn he had left early and had gone fishing. She would never have gone fishing in the middle of the week.

Still, in spite of their differences, Carol sincerely hoped that some kind of relationship could evolve between them. Harlan was the nicest man she had met in a long time, and if Brandon was anything like his father, Carol could understand why Kim had wanted so desperately to marry the young man.

Carol was just clipping on her large gold earrings when the

doorbell rang. "Do we have time for a drink?" she asked as she opened the door to Harlan.

"No, but we do have time for a kiss," Harlan said as he tipped her face up and kissed her lips firmly. Carol put her hands on his shoulders and kissed him back, the attraction between them flaring once again. Harlan stared down into her eyes as he traced a line under her eye with his finger. "No tired circles tonight," he said approvingly. "Good day at work?"

"Yes, for once," Carol said, biting her lip when she realized what her words implied.

Harlan acted as if he didn't hear her. "We better get going," he said as Carol locked the door behind them. "Kimberly and Brand are probably starving by now."

"I'm sure they are."

Carol and Harlan talked all the way to their children's apartment. Kim had called Carol just a few days ago and had told her all about her courses and her professors and college life in general, and Carol was delighted that Kim seemed to be enjoying her studies. Harlan had put Brandon over his own team of trimmers, and he admitted that he missed working with his son, although he was proud that Brandon could handle that responsibility at such a young age. They were both smiling as they climbed the stairs to Kim and Brandon's apartment, but they froze outside the door at the sound of raised, angry voices inside.

Carol reached out and quickly knocked on the door. A moment later Brandon jerked the door open as he tried to rearrange his scowl into a smile.

"Hi," he said, trying to sound friendly and not quite making it.

"Hello," Carol said gravely, looking from Brandon's face to Kim's and then up at Harlan. Apparently they had walked in on a major battle. "How are you tonight?"

"Tired," Kim said quietly. "Would you be hurt if I didn't go out with you this evening?"

"Are you all right?" Carol asked anxiously.

"No, she's not all right," Brandon snapped. "She's worn to a frazzle from her schedule, but she's too hard-headed to do the sensible thing and quit until the baby's born."

"I'm not about to quit!" Kim snapped back at him. "So you can take all your stupid ideas and shove 'em!" Kim turned to Carol, tears in her eyes. "He wants me to quit, Mom. Can you believe that?"

"I didn't say you had to quit forever, damn it!" Brandon said angrily. "Just until after the baby comes. Is that too much to ask?"

Carol opened her mouth, but Kim spoke first. "*Yes,* it's too much, Brandon! You promised me you'd help me through college, and now you're reneging on me. That's not fair!"

"I'm worried about you!" Brandon said. "I'm worried about you and the baby."

"Maybe Brandon's right," Harlan said, his face solemn. "Maybe Kim should drop out until after the baby comes. It would be easier for her and the baby."

"Like hell!" Carol snapped, her eyes blazing with anger. "Brandon, I thought you and I got this straight the night I agreed to your marriage. Kim was going to stay in school and get her education. You promised me, Brandon, and you're going to live up to that promise or I'm taking her back home. Do you understand?"

Brandon's eyes widened as Harlan's narrowed.

"Carol, don't be ridiculous!" Harlan snapped. "She's not going home with you."

"Don't bet on it, Harlan," Kim said bitterly. "I don't care how tired I am. I want my education more than either of you will ever understand. He's standing in my way."

"Kim, I am *not* standing in your way," Brandon said. "I just want you to drop out until the baby's born. Is that too much to ask?"

"Yes, it is," Kim said vehemently.

"Why?" Brandon asked, bewildered.

"Because it won't stop there, Brandon," Carol said bitterly.

"The baby will come, and then you won't want her to go off and leave it with a babysitter, and then you'll want another child, and then you'll need a little extra money and Kim will have to go to work at a dead-end job, and the next thing you know ten or fifteen years of her life will be gone. My daughter deserves better than that. If she drops out now, she'll never get her education."

"That's the most ridiculous thing I've ever heard," Harlan said. "Brandon isn't trying to hold her back, just keep her from wearing herself out. I think she should drop out."

"Who asked you?" Carol snapped sarcastically. "What do you know about getting an education, anyway?"

Harlan visibly winced. "Enough to know that it's not worth Kim's killing herself or risking my unborn grandchild for," he said angrily. "Kim, you can go back later."

"No," Kim said stubbornly. "If Brandon won't help me, I'll do it without him. Mom, I'm coming home with you tonight." She went into the bedroom and got out her suitcase.

"Kim, you can't do that!" Brandon said angrily. "Carol, you're not taking her home with you."

"No, I'm not," Carol said calmly. "But I'm sure not barring the door to her if she comes of her own free will. Brandon, can't you see? You're breaking your promise to me and Kim."

"If your daughter weren't so damn mule-headed, and you weren't so fanatic about a piece of sheepskin, there wouldn't be a problem, so don't lay the blame at Brandon's door," Harlan said angrily.

Carol lifted her nose ever so slightly. "Harlan, I can't expect you to understand why this is so important to Kim and me. But it is, and both of you are going to have to learn to respect that."

Kim carried her large suitcase from the bedroom. She handed the suitcase to Carol and gathered up her books and notebook. "Let's go," she said, sweeping past Harlan and Brandon.

Carol followed Kim out the door, her back as straight as Kim's as they walked out to Kim's car. Kim opened the passenger side and handed Carol the keys. "I'm not up to fighting the traffic," she said as she collapsed in the seat.

Carol backed out of the parking space. "This isn't right, you know," she said quietly. "You shouldn't be running home to me."

"Too bad." Kim's jaw jutted forward stubbornly. "Brandon's being unreasonable."

"Kim, is college really wearing you out?" Carol asked anxiously. "If you're working to hard, maybe Brandon has a point."

"It's not college, Mom, or at least I don't think it is. I love school."

"But are you tired?"

"Of course. Wouldn't you be if you had dinner and laundry and cleaning to do every day when you got home?"

"You were doing all that too?" Carol asked incredulously. "Wasn't Brandon doing any of it?"

"No, he wasn't."

"Why not?"

Kim shrugged. "I guess he never thought about it. I was home all summer and did it then."

"Didn't you ask him to help you?"

"No, I never asked," Kim said quietly.

Carol let out the breath she had been holding. Kim and Brandon were suffering from a youthful lack of communication, aggravated by a different set of values. "Tell you what. You let him think about it tonight, and then tomorrow you and Brandon can talk. If he refuses to help you, take it from there." Carol doubted that the boy would refuse to help Kim once she had asked him to.

"Thanks for letting me come, Mom," Kim said softly. "I'm sorry we involved you and Harlan. Although I don't think he understands, either."

"Neither do I," Carol said, "although he might once he realizes what the problem is. But Harlan was right, you know. I am interfering tonight by letting you come home."

"My heart bleeds," Kim said dryly.

Carol parked Kim's car in the driveway, and Kim disappeared into her old bedroom and shut the door behind her. Carol peeked in a little later, expecting to find Kim in tears, and instead found her bent over a textbook, eagerly reading and marking her text with a yellow felt-tipped pen. And that foolish boy wanted her to drop out! She only hoped that Brandon would learn to understand Kim's new-found passion for her studies.

Kim studied until late into the night and was still sleeping the next morning when Carol heard a sharp knock on the front door. She put down her coffee and the morning paper to answer, finding a tight-lipped Brandon standing on the front step.

"I've come to take my wife home," he said firmly. "And I've come to tell you to stop interfering in my marriage."

"Tough." Carol looked at him with a hard, unyielding expression on her face. "You don't demand anything of me while you're standing on my front porch."

"My father said—"

"I'm not scared of you and I'm not scared of your father," Carol said coldly. "Do you extend a little courtesy to me or do I slam this door in your face, the way I should have done a year ago?"

Brandon swallowed. "May I come in?"

Carol opened the door and Brandon followed her into the living room. "Sit down. I have a few things I want to say to you."

Brandon looked belligerent, but he sat.

"I will be the first one to admit that I'm interfering in your marriage," she began.

Brandon looked surprised at the admission. "Then you do admit that you're interfering."

"I admit it, but I don't apologize for it. And furthermore, I fully intend to interfere any time you jeopardize the future of my grandchild, so you either better start thinking of that little baby or get used to a lot of interference from me."

"How am I jeopardizing the baby's future?" Brandon demanded.

"By asking Kim to drop out of school," Carol answered. "Because if she does drop out, she'll be years going back, if ever."

"But what does that have to do with the baby?" Brandon asked. "I can take care of them."

"Sure, as long as you're married," Carol said. She sat down across from Brandon and lit a cigarette. "But let's suppose that something happens to your marriage, and Kim has to go out and support that baby alone. She'd earn minimum wage checking groceries or cleaning somebody's house."

"But I'm not going to divorce her," Brandon protested.

"You hope you don't, but you don't know that. Then too, it's a horrible thought, but you could die young, Brandon, or be disabled. You of all people should know that, after what happened to your mother. And where would that leave Kim?"

"It wouldn't be so bad, would it?"

"Has Kim ever told you what it was like for her after her father and I divorced and I was trying to finish school?" Carol asked quietly.

"No, she's never said anything."

"She probably hasn't said anything because she's being loyal to me, but that period of time was really hard on her, Brandon. Money was very tight. We lived on hot dogs and macaroni and cheese, and the only new clothes she got that year and a half were the clothes her grandmother bought her. And on the days I was late and she couldn't stay with the neighbors next door, she had to open up the house and stay by herself. It didn't happen often, but she was scared and she hated it every time it did happen."

Brandon swallowed. "She never told me any of that."

"Why do you think she's so determined to get her education now?" Carol demanded. "I'm not the one pushing her to stay in school, although I'm sure you and your father would disagree."

Brandon turned a bright shade of red. "But what am I supposed to do?" he asked. "She's worn out!"

"You could get up off your lazy butt and help her a little around the apartment," Carol said. "That's what's wearing her out. Not school."

"But I work hard trimming every day," Brandon said.

"Oh, Brandon," Carol said disgustedly. "Honestly, expecting her to do all the cooking and cleaning and laundry while she's going to school is too much. Who did the housework after your mother died?"

"Dad hired a maid," Brandon said defensively. "I don't even know how to clean a house!"

"Well, if you don't think enough of her to help her around the apartment," Carol said, "I'll hire a maid for you so she can finish her education."

Brandon's shoulders sagged. "You have a way of making a man feel about an inch and a half tall," he said quietly. "But you're right—I should have realized that she needed help."

"Then will you help her, and stop hounding her to quit school?" Carol asked quietly. "Brandon, I've never seen her this enthusiastic about school before, and I'm honestly afraid of what she might do if you demand that she give it up. Kim took that promise you made to me very seriously."

"Would she put her education before me?" Brandon asked bitterly.

"Would you back her into that corner?"

"No. I'm scared to," Brandon admitted.

"Brandon, I know she loves you, but college is important to her too," Carol said gently. "Help her with it, and she'll love you that much more."

"Brandon, is that you?" Kim asked from the door of the living room. She stared at him warily, her hair tousled and her robe barely covering her swollen figure.

"Yes, it's me." Brandon stood up and faced his wife. "Kim, I'm sorry. I didn't know you needed help with the housework."

Kim shrugged.

"Will you come home with me?"

"Will you stop bugging me to quit school?" Kim asked.

"Yeah, I'll quit bugging you," Brandon said. "Will you be home in a little while?"

"I'll be out in a few minutes." Kim went back to her bedroom and shut the door.

"I think she's still mad," Brandon said.

"Why don't you get her to show you how to clean the bathroom?" Carol suggested. "That will put her in a good mood very quickly!"

"All right," Brandon said. "I'm sorry we dragged you and Dad into this."

"I am too," she said quietly.

Carol offered to cook Kim and Brandon breakfast, but Brandon said that he would take Kim out to eat before he went home for his first housekeeping lesson. Carol ate a piece of toast and started cleaning her house, her mind still on the argument of the night before. She hoped that Brandon would make good on his promise to help Kim out around the house and stop trying to get her to drop out of school. Carol was opposed to the idea herself, but she sensed that Kim was even more opposed to leaving her studies, even temporarily. Carol was afraid that continued pressure from Brandon and his father would only create more stormy times in the future.

She was dusting the coffee table when the doorbell rang. She peeked out the window and her lips firmed when she spotted Harlan's car in the driveway. He's probably come to tell the witch to get off her broom, Carol thought grimly. If he had, he was about to get a piece of her mind too.

Carol opened the front door. "Where's Kim?" Harlan demanded. "I want to talk to her."

"She's gone home."

"Good. I guess Brandon talked some sense into her."

Carol shrugged. "He apologized for being a jerk and went home for a lesson in housekeeping, if that amounts to talking some sense into her." Her eyes were angry as she stared into Harlan's. "She's not leaving college, Harlan."

"Damn it, Carol, stop interfering in those kids' lives!" he snapped. "Let me in so we can talk about this."

"I'll tell you the same thing I told your insolent son," Carol said sharply. "You don't stand at my front door and demand anything. If you want to come into my home and talk to me, you ask."

"Carol, we have to talk. This is serious. Let me in. Please."

Reluctantly, Carol opened the door wider. Harlan pushed past her and sat down on the sofa in the family room. "Carol, you've simply got to stop interfering in Brand and Kim's life," he demanded as Carol sat down across from him. "If you don't, you're going to ruin that marriage. Besides, how long do you think Brand's going to let you tell him how to run his life?"

"He'll let me as long as I'm right," Carol said. "And I am on this. He admitted as much this morning before he apologized to my daughter. Furthermore, I'm not the only one around here interfering, am I?" she taunted. "I gathered that you and Brandon had a little talk last night after we left. Not only are you trying to interfere, but you're out to ruin my daughter's life. I don't like that, and I don't think that Kim does, either."

"Out to ruin her life?" Harlan demanded. "How am I out to do that? I'm worried about her, for crying out loud! She's seven months pregnant and trying to go to school and take care of an apartment by herself."

"That's exactly the problem," Carol said. "If you hadn't raised your son to be such a typical male, she wouldn't be so worn out from taking care of the housework on her own. That's the problem, Harlan, not her studies."

Harlan held up his hands in a conciliatory gesture. "All right, I can see the sense in that, and I'm sure now that Brand's had the error of his ways pointed out to him, he'll help her more. But I still don't understand why you and Kim are both so hell-bent on her staying in school this semester, when it would probably be better for her to be out."

Carol sighed. "Don't you understand, Harlan? She wants an education, and if she quits now, it will take her years to get one, if she ever does."

"You're only thinking of Kim," Harlan accused her. "You're not thinking of the baby she's carrying."

"Like hell!" Carol snapped. "Just who do you think I am thinking of? What would happen to that baby if anything ever happened to that marriage and Kim didn't have an education? Or what would happen to that child if Brandon was disabled or died young?" Unconsciously Carol's face became bitter. "Or what do you think it's going to be like for that child if somewhere down the road Kim starts to resent Brandon because she had to interrupt her education at his insistence?"

"Like you resented Venson?" Harlan asked quietly.

"Of course," Carol said instantly, her voice bitter.

"You've infected that girl with your own bitterness," Harlan said tightly. "She's terrified to drop out even for a semester because of you."

"If she's bitter, it's because her father left me before I could support her. You think she's always had fancy clothes and a sports car? Harlan, we lived below the poverty level for a year and a half, because even if I'd wanted to quit school and go to work, I wasn't qualified to do a damned thing to support her. She lived on macaroni and hot dogs and had a key on a string around her neck. Maybe she doesn't want that to happen to her baby someday."

"But what is her insistence on an education going to do to their marriage if she's so determined on school that she won't even drop out for a semester when she's pregnant?" Harlan demanded. "It could destroy it, you know."

"Ask the opposite question," Carol said quietly. "You better wonder what's going to happen to that marriage if she doesn't get her education. What do you think destroyed mine? A lot of what went wrong between Jack and me was the fact that I resented the hell out of having to quit school. I don't want that to happen to Kim."

Harlan shook his head slowly. "I can't believe it! You and Kim both put an education above everything else—even your marriages and the health of an unborn child. And an education's not worth that, Carol. Nothing's worth that."

"You're wrong, Harlan," Carol said vehemently. "An education's worth everything."

Harlan and Carol stared bitterly into one another's eyes for a moment before Harlan walked out and slammed the door behind him. Carol shut her eyes and leaned back into her chair as disappointment brought tears to her eyes. There was no way she and Harlan could ever have a relationship—she knew that now. This argument had shown her that they were just too different, that they would never be able to reach a compromise between his philosophy and hers.

Carol leaned back in the chair as two tears trickled down her cheeks. She had hoped that something, she wasn't sure what, might come of their relationship. She had let herself daydream about a warm and loving affair with Harlan, maybe even marriage someday. He could have run his business and she could have pursued her career, and together they could have watched their grandchild grow up. But now that was out. If his values were so different from hers that he couldn't understand why Kim needed to stay in school, then they didn't have any future together. Carol wiped her face and dried her eyes and went on with her housework, but that special sparkle that had been in her life for the last month was completely gone.

Harlan pulled up in front of Kim and Brandon's apartment and climbed the stairs, listening for the sounds of quarreling from inside. Though Kim had agreed to go home with Brandon, Harlan couldn't quite believe that everything had been straightened out that easily. He was sure Carol had chewed Brandon out that morning, probably more harshly than she had yelled at him, and he wondered how his headstrong son had taken the tongue-lashing. And he still wasn't convinced that Kim had any business being in school, if she was as tired as she had been last night. He simply couldn't understand why Carol and Kim were both so determined that Kim had to stay in college.

Harlan knocked and a moment later Kim answered, her thumb in a book and a yellow marking pen between her teeth. " 'Lo," she said around the marker. She took it out of her mouth. "Hi, come on in," she said, holding the door wider. "Brandon, it's your dad."

Brandon stepped out of the kitchen, a dishtowel in his hands. "Hi, Dad. Kim, where does the frying pan go?"

"In the cabinet on the right of the sink," Kim said. "Sit down, Harlan, and I'll get you a beer."

"Thanks, I could use one," Harlan said as she went into the kitchen.

Kim handed him a beer and turned her book upside down on the couch as they sat down. "I don't want to lose my place," she explained. "Economics is fascinating." Her eyes snapped with an enthusiasm Harlan didn't miss.

"I'm sure it's interesting," Harlan said. "Is it your favorite course?"

Kim shrugged. "I love them all," she admitted. "It's like—I don't know, there's so much out there just waiting for me to learn. Economics, history, biology—I don't know which one's more fascinating." Kim stopped and laughed self-consciously. "I guess I sound like a typical college freshman, don't I? But I do like it, Harlan."

She would have to, Harlan thought ruefully, to have that kind of enthusiasm when she's seven months pregnant and worn out.

Brandon came out and sat down beside Kim. "All finished," he said. "Was there anything you wanted, Dad?"

"Uh, nothing, I just thought I would come by and say hello," Harlan lied feebly.

The phone rang and Kim went in the bedroom to answer it.

"Yes, Dad, everything's fine," Brandon said dryly. "Kim's

going to stay in school and I'm going to try to help her out more around here."

"But do you think that's the best thing for her?" Harlan asked. "Shouldn't she be taking it a little easier?"

"Maybe she should, but she isn't going to," Brandon said quietly. "She's determined to go to school, and like her sharp-tongued mama told me, Kim's going to love me a lot more if I support her in it."

"You don't think her mother's pushing her?" Harlan asked.

"Her mother's behind her, all right, but the pushing's all on Kim's part." Brandon looked over at Harlan, his eyes worried. "She's changing, Dad. She didn't care this much in high school."

Kim came out of the bedroom laughing. "Mother's blunter than you are, Harlan. She came out and asked if we'd made up and if everything was all right."

Harlan laughed. "Am I that transparent? Yes, I was worried and I'm glad everything's straightened out."

Harlan stayed a few more minutes and finished his beer. He got in the car and started to go home, but he found himself heading toward Carol's house instead.

Carol was answering a stack of correspondence when the doorbell rang. She bit her lip when she looked out the peephole and saw Harlan standing there. She knew she had to talk to him sometime, but she hadn't wanted to do it that night. She opened the door and stared into his eyes. "Good evening," she said gravely as she stepped aside so he could enter.

Harlan stepped in and closed the door behind him. Carol gestured toward the family room and he sat down in his usual chair.

"I thought you might be worried about the kids," he said. "I just left there and they've apparently settled their differences."

"That's good to hear," Carol said quietly. "I wouldn't want to see them fighting all the time."

"I still don't like the idea of her staying in school," Harlan admitted. "I worry about her too, Carol, not just the baby."

"Kim will be fine," Carol said calmly. "I think she or her doctor could tell if she were endangering herself or the baby in any way."

"I hope so," Harlan said doubtfully. "Have you had dinner? We could try that little place near the Galleria that just opened up."

"I don't think so, Harlan," Carol said.

Harlan looked up at the final, regretful tone in her voice. "Out with it."

"I don't want to continue seeing you, Harlan. Oh, I know we'll have to see one another now and then because of the kids and the baby, but I don't think it would be wise for us to continue dating."

"Why not?" he demanded. "Are you still angry with me for what I said this morning?"

"Not angry, Harlan. You have a right to your feelings and opinions, just as I have. But the disagreement, and the fact that you still don't understand why it's crucial for Kim to stay in school right now, no matter how hard it might be on her for a while, only goes to show that our basic values are just too different for us to carry on with this relationship. It would be better if we broke it off now."

"That's ridiculous!" Harlan retorted. "Just because we disagree on whether Kim ought to stay in school is no reason for us to break off what we have going."

"But we're not just disagreeing on whether or not Kim ought to stay in school," Carol argued quietly. "We're not just fighting about her health and that of her baby. We're arguing over the importance of an education to my daughter's future. We're arguing over the importance of an education and a career, period. And if we disagree on something that fundamental, we haven't got a chance for any kind of happy relationship."

"Carol, you can't mean that!" Harlan snapped, his eyes angry. "You can't honestly be that upset because I don't happen to think an education's all that important."

"Yes, I can be that upset!" Carol cried. "Because if you don't think an education's all that important, then you can't believe that a career's all that important, either. And that leaves us with nothing in common, because I believe that both are vital. Look, I'm disappointed and I'm sorry, but if we kept seeing each other and let this relationship go in the direction it's headed, we'd only make each other miserable."

"After what we've shared, how can you sit there and tell me we don't have anything in common?" Harlan demanded. He stood and pulled her out of her chair to face him. "What about the movies, the dancing, the fun we had?" He held her forearms tightly. "What about this?" he asked as he bent his head and ground his lips into hers.

Carol gasped and tried to pull away, but Harlan held her nape tightly as he plundered her lips with his, taking her sweetness as he offered her his own. Carol tried to resist, but she was her own worst enemy. She felt her mouth softening, and slowly, as Harlan used all the sensual persuasion he was capable of, she opened her lips to him, falling further and further under his spell. His tongue sought and found the sensitive tip of hers, their passionate duel further inflaming Carol's soaring desire. Gradually her arms crept around his waist and she held him as his free hand slid down her back, sending shivers along her spine. She gasped when he released her lips only to nibble at her temple lightly, persuading her without words that she wanted him.

Carol forgot everything except that she wanted him. She ran her hands down his hard, warm back, touching the ridged muscles with eager, hungry fingers. A part of her wanted to make love to Harlan so badly she ached. A part of her wanted to pull his clothes from his body, to feel his nakedness close to her and to share herself totally with him. She groaned when his hand dipped and he stroked her bottom. She could feel that he wanted her as badly as she wanted him, even if it was all wrong for them otherwise.

Harlan pulled away and stared down at her, his eyes glittering. "I'd say we have a lot in common, don't you?" he rasped.

Carol looked up at him as tears formed in her eyes. "But sex isn't enough, Harlan."

Harlan cursed as he thrust her from him. "Call me when you come to your senses," he said harshly. For the second time that day, Harlan slammed the front door behind him when he left.

Carol stared out the window as the taillights of his car disappeared into the darkness. Yes, they had a powerful physical attraction between them, but apparently that was all they had in common. Carol reached up and felt her lips. They still tingled from the force of Harlan's sensual embrace, but he wasn't so rough that she would have bruises in the morning. If he had kissed her and caressed her for just a few minutes more that night, she would have willingly become his. And Carol was almost sorry that he hadn't forced the issue.

Almost, but not quite. She returned to her desk, but instead of answering the inquiry about Zero Coupons she had in front of her, she stared into space and thought about what she had done that night. She had to admit that no man had ever drawn the same kind of sensual response from her that Harlan had. But that wasn't enough for Carol—if she and Harlan couldn't agree on more than sex, their relationship was doomed, and it was better to break it off now. Carol's eyes filled with unshed tears, and the letter wavered in front of her. She knew she was going to miss Harlan, but she also knew she wasn't going to be making that call.

CHAPTER SEVEN

Carol put the finishing touches on her makeup and stared at herself in the mirror. She hoped she wasn't overdressed in her designer jeans and a silk blouse, but she hadn't been to a teen-age birthday party in a long time, and since she and Scott were going out afterward, she had to dress for that as well. Kim was celebrating her eighteenth birthday that night, and she had graciously invited her mother to come. Carol feared Harlan was going to be there also, but she knew they would have to see one another sooner or later, and that night was as good a time as any. Satisfied that she looked fine, Carol wandered into the kitchen and poured herself a club soda.

Taking her drink out to the patio, she stood looking at the trees, thinking of all the work Harlan and Brandon had done on them. Before she could stop herself, she thought about how Harlan had looked that day without his shirt and how his hard body had felt held tightly against hers. She had missed Harlan terribly the last few weeks, especially now that she was no longer angry with him for his attitude toward Kim's education. Kim had told her just yesterday that Harlan had said no more about her dropping out for the semester, so he had apparently accepted Kim's desire to stay in school.

But Carol had not been tempted to pick up the telephone and call Harlan. Though he may have accepted Kim's decision, Carol was convinced that he really didn't understand it, nor did he understand why Carol was so adamant about it. And if he couldn't understand that, she felt that their values were just too different for them to make a go of any kind of intimate relationship. They would only make one another miserable, and Carol didn't want that. So she willed herself not to think about him and had started seeing Scott again in an effort to get on with her life. Maybe the earth didn't move when Scott kissed her, but at least they understood one another.

Carol finished her drink and drove to Kim and Brandon's apartment. She laughed as she parked—she could see and hear signs of the party from the parking lot. Kim had reserved the party room of the complex for tonight, and a keg outside the door was surrounded by a group of young men. Mercifully, the music was at a fairly tolerable level, although Carol suspected it would get louder once the older generation had said their goodbyes. Kim met her at the door and enveloped her in a big hug. "Thanks," she said as Carol handed her a gaily wrapped present. "Do I get to open it now?"

"No, I'm going to make you wait until midnight," Carol teased. "Of course you can open it."

Kim quickly tore off the paper and withdrew a warm wool jacket.

"There should be a pair of gloves in there too," Carol said.

"Mom, this is the greatest," Kim said as she held up the coat. "Thanks so much."

"Those are really nice," Harlan said over her shoulder.

"Thank you," Carol replied, hoping she sounded normal. Harlan's deep voice affected her more than she wanted it to. Plastering a smile on her face, she extended her hand. "It's good to see you tonight."

Harlan clasped her hand briefly. "It's good to see you too," he said softly, only his eyes betraying his sarcasm.

Carol stuck her chin out just a little as Harlan turned to Kim. "I didn't know what to get you," he said as he handed her an envelope.

Kim tore open the envelope and stared down at a check. "Gosh, Harlan, thanks," she said. "You really didn't have to."

"That's not what Brandon said," Harlan teased. He turned to Carol. "Are you alone tonight?" he asked sardonically.

"Yes. Are you?" Carol shot back.

"Obviously. I thought you would have brought that fancy lawyer you used to see all the time."

"As a matter of fact, Scott and I have a date later this evening. A teenager's birthday party doesn't interest him all that much," Carol said.

"I'm going out too," Harlan said softly.

"I hope you have a good time," Carol said graciously, fighting back a ridiculous feeling of jealousy. She didn't want Harlan, and it was silly for her to feel jealous of him.

She got up abruptly and went over to the table, where Kim had laid out an array of snacks. She took a little food on her plate and sat down with Kim, across the room from Harlan.

"It was really nice of you to come for a little while this evening," Kim said. "You could have gone out with Scott. I wouldn't have minded."

"I wouldn't miss your party for the world," Carol assured her. "And Scott was more than glad to make it a late date. How's school going? Have you gotten any of your midterms back?"

Kim smiled shyly. "Straight A's, Mom. I aced every test."

"Kimberly, that's marvelous!" Carol cried. "Have you told Brandon?"

"You mean has the curvebuster shown me her scores?" Brandon teased as he sat down beside Kim. "She's even shown me the tests. She made a perfect score on one of them."

"I knew you were bright, Kim, but even I didn't realize you were capable of that kind of work," Carol said quietly. "I'm so pleased." Her eyes gleamed wickedly. "I can hardly wait to tell Bennie Johnson! He's proud of the B's and C's his boy is making."

"Uh-oh, do I detect a little parental rivalry somewhere?" Harlan said as he sat down across from Brandon, balancing a plate of food on his knee.

"Mom and Mr. Johnson have been at it for the last three years," Kim said. "You've probably heard of his son, Ronnie Johnson. Ronnie's playing football at Texas A&M now."

Harlan nodded. "So what are you going to hit the poor man with Monday, Carol?"

"Kim's making straight A's at the moment," Carol said proudly.

"That's wonderful, Kim," Harlan said warmly. "I'm sure it must be quite a challenge to make those kinds of grades."

Kim shook her head slightly. "But that's the funny part—it isn't, really. Once I got interested and started applying myself, the work turned out to be really easy. In fact, I'm thinking about looking into a scholarship next fall to Rice, if my grades stay this good. I might find Rice more of a challenge."

"Kim, do you mean it? Are you really thinking of going there?" Carol asked delightedly. "That would be wonderful. Rice graduates have an excellent crack at graduate school and all the professional schools."

"Is that true?" Harlan asked quietly.

"Absolutely," Carol said firmly. "I don't care what they say about equality, a degree from a prestigious university like Rice is a ticket in the door of a lot of places. Scott's degree from Rice really helped him get into law school."

Kim got up to put out more chips, and Carol turned to Brandon and Harlan. "Wouldn't it be wonderful if she went there?" she asked.

Brandon shrugged. "I'm barely affording U of H," he said unenthusiastically.

"Brandon, I'm not sure, but I think that Rice sometimes adjusts their tuition to what you can pay," Carol said gently, sensing that Brandon wasn't really very pleased with Kim's plans. "I doubt that it would cost that much more for her to go there."

"I hope not," Brandon said, and Carol and Harlan were left in no doubt that Brandon, for one, wasn't enthusiastic about Rice.

Brandon got up when more of Kim's friends came through the door, leaving Harlan and Carol seated together. "I'm glad Kim's doing so well," he said softly.

"Are you really?"

Harlan's face turned a little red. "Yes, I am," he said. "I'm not ashamed to admit that I was wrong about something—unlike some people I know."

Carol's lips compressed into a thin line. "I can't imagine who." She rose abruptly. "It was good to see you, Harlan," she said shortly.

"Likewise," he retorted sarcastically.

Carol sought out Kim and Brandon. "Kim, thanks for having me," she said.

"I wouldn't think of not having you," Kim said as she hugged her mother. "And thanks for the coat."

Harlan came up behind Carol. "I think I better be going also," he said. "I'll leave you kids to it."

Brandon thanked them again for coming, and Harlan followed Carol out to the parking lot. "Have a good time," he said.

"You too," Carol replied.

Carol swore as she checked her watch and rushed home, irritated with Harlan and herself for letting him get to her and irritated because she was going to be late for her date with Scott. Scott's car was in the driveway and he was sitting on the front porch when she arrived.

"How was the party?" he asked, as he met her and helped her into his car.

"Wonderful," Carol said dryly.

"What's the matter? Did all that awful music get to you?" he teased as he backed out of the driveway.

"No, I hardly noticed the music. Kim's father-in-law was there," she said.

"Ah. How was Mr. Macho? Still want to keep Kim home barefoot and pregnant?" Carol had given Scott an abbreviated version of the kids' fight and her and Harlan's part in it, but she had failed to mention that she and Harlan had been seeing one another.

"No, apparently he's softened a little on that," Carol said thoughtfully.

"So what's the problem?" Scott persisted. "Surely you can tolerate a blue-collar chauvinist for a little while without blowing your cool."

"Harlan's not a blue-collar chauvinist," Carol protested quickly. "He's really very intelligent." She blushed when she realized what she had said.

Scott turned surprised eyes in her direction, and when he saw her blush, his face split into a huge grin. "My, God, I can't believe it! You're sticking up for the guy! Dare I ask how you spent that month you were suddenly out of circulation?"

"I dated Harlan a few times," Carol said tightly. "What's the big deal?"

Scott started to laugh even harder. "What on earth did you find to talk about?"

"The same things I talk about with you," she replied tartly. "Just because he's not educated doesn't mean he's stupid."

Scott pulled into the parking lot of his favorite restaurant, a noisy place with lots of wood and brass. There were no tables available, so they waited in the bar and Scott ordered a drink.

"I can't believe you actually dated Harlan Stone," he said, grinning wickedly. "Why? Was it a kick to go with somebody completely different from your usual type?"

Carol turned exasperated eyes to him. "Don't be such a snob, Scott. I really liked the man, all right?"

His grin faded. "So what happened to make you run back to good old Scott?"

"A difference in values, I guess," she admitted. "I told you about that fight the kids had that we got involved in. Even though he's given in, Harlan simply can't understand why Kim's education is so important—he actually agreed with Brandon that she should drop out for the semester! I decided right then that his outlook on life was just too different from mine to sustain any kind of intimate relationship, which was the direction we were headed."

"So you sent him packing."

"So I sent him packing."

"You're probably right," Scott said as he lit Carol's cigarette. "But it hurt you, didn't it?"

"Yes, it did," Carol said softly. "No offense, Scott, but he was the first man since the divorce I could see myself getting serious about."

"Are you sure your differences are that great?" he asked gently. "A lot of people disagree on the value of a college education."

"I think they are," Carol said stubbornly, and Scott knew better than to try to change her mind. Scott's name came over the loudspeaker, and they found the headwaiter and were escorted to their table.

Scott wanted to hear a new jazz group playing at one of the highrise hotel bars, so it was late when they finally turned onto Carol's street.

"My God, what's Harlan doing parked out in front of the house?" Carol asked. "I hope nothing's happened to the kids."

Scott smiled as he pulled into the driveway. They got out of the car and Harlan immediately met her.

"Where the hell have you been?" he demanded.

"Out with my date," Carol said. "Where's yours?"

"I took Frannie home," Harlan said tightly. "Ryan, go on home. Carol and I need to talk."

Carol eyed Harlan suspiciously. She couldn't smell any liquor, and he certainly didn't seem drunk, but he was behaving out of character and she didn't particularly want to be alone with him. "I think I said everything I had to say last month," she said quietly. "Save us both a lot of embarrassment and go home."

"I want to talk to you," he said firmly. "And I'd like to do it privately. So would you get rid of your fancy friend here?"

Carol glanced over at Scott, who was staring at Harlan with

cool amusement. "Is this the way you blue-collar boys win friends and influence people?" he asked.

"Ryan, I said to get the hell out of here," Harlan repeated through clenched teeth.

"I'm not leaving Carol alone with a wild-eyed maniac. Or is this just that macho hype you physical types are so famous for?" Scott goaded.

"What would you know about macho?" Harlan said tauntingly. "You fancy professionals have it all upstairs and nothing below." He stared at Scott's lithe body contemptuously as Carol bit her lip nervously. Harlan was a good two inches taller than Scott and quite a bit heavier. "Sit on your butt at that fancy college, did you? I bet you can't lift anything heavier than a pencil, Ryan. And you're going to protect her from me?"

Scott's lips tightened. Suddenly his fist shot out, and Harlan was sprawled in the middle of the yard, flat on his back.

"My God, what have you done to him, Scott?" Carol cried, astonishment mingling with horror in her voice. She knelt beside Harlan and slapped his face lightly. "Harlan, are you all right?" she asked anxiously.

Harlan pushed himself up and stared at his adversary groggily. Scott grinned down at them as he straightened his coat. "We had a boxing team at Rice," he said softly. "You have a lot to learn about professional men, Stone." He looked from Harlan to Carol. "I think you'd both be a lot happier if you went in the house and talked things over," he added. "Night, Carol."

Harlan stared as Scott pulled out of the driveway. "Jeez, I didn't know he could do that."

"Neither did I," Carol said softly. She looked at Harlan's rapidly swelling eye. "You look terrible. Come on in, and I'll give you a compress for that eye."

Groaning, Harlan pushed himself up from the ground and followed Carol into the house. "Good grief, your friend packs a wallop," he said as he looked in the mirror.

"You shouldn't have come on so strong with him," Carol

scolded as she got a couple of ice cubes out of the icemaker and wrapped them in a dishtowel. "Professional men are constantly having their masculinity challenged and most of them are dying for a chance to prove it. Why do you think the weight rooms at the health clubs are full of them?"

Harlan took the towel and sat down at the kitchen table. "He wasn't above a little name-calling himself," Harlan replied. "Oh, God, that hurts!" he said as he eased the towel over his eye.

Carol poured him a drink without being asked and set it in front of him. Harlan sipped it gratefully. "I'll never challenge a yuppie again," he said. "I guess I was wrong to taunt him. . . . I'm sorry, Carol. It's just that I was so jealous that I could have cheerfully broken his neck. Or at least tried to." Harlan hung his head morosely. "He's everything you want in a man and everything I can't be. He's got a fancy education, a profession, and I bet he makes more than you do, doesn't he?"

"A lot more," Carol admitted. "But what's this I'm hearing from you, Harlan? I thought you were perfectly content with your life-style. Since when have you started envying the Scotts of the world?"

"Since you chose him over me," Harlan said. "It really shook me when you gave me my walking papers last month. I thought we had something special going, and then you went back to him."

"But I stopped seeing him in order to make time to date you." Carol stroked Harlan's forearm. "And I only started seeing him again after you and I quarreled."

Harlan took the towel off his eye. "How does it look?"

"Put the towel back on."

Harlan held the towel back up. "I've thought a lot about things these last few weeks," he said quietly. "And I've watched Kim—she really loves going to school. I hate admitting it, but I was wrong about her. She was right to insist on staying in. She has as much right to an education as she would have if she had stayed single, and she's wise to get it now, while she's still young."

Carol was silent for a minute. "What changed your mind? When you walked out of here last month, you were convinced that she and I placed too much emphasis on her education."

"Watching Kim, partly, and talking to my sister-in-law. She's trying to juggle school and three school-age kids. Laura wants to go so badly, and it's three times as hard for her now. But she's determined to get her degree in nursing. Carol, until I talked to her, I never realized what a difference an education makes in a woman's earning power. Anyway, it didn't take me very long to figure out that I was wrong about Kim's education."

"So where have you been for the last few weeks?" Carol asked quietly.

"I wasn't sure you wanted me to come back around," Harlan admitted. "You were pretty definite that night when you told me to take a hike. I thought you had decided that you preferred men with an education and a profession like yours."

"Not necessarily," Carol said.

Harlan's head jerked up. "Does that mean you'll start seeing me again?"

Carol bit her lip. "I don't know," she said. "I'll be honest and admit that I've missed you horribly, but I'm still not sure you and I can make a go of a relationship."

"Look, I've admitted that I was wrong—very wrong—to assume that Kim's education wasn't all that important. And I'll do everything I can to help her stay in school. I've already offered to pay her spring tuition, but Brandon insists that he can afford it."

"You did that?" Carol asked. "But I can afford to send her, if they would just let me."

"Yes, but Brandon might take it from me, even if he's too proud to take it from you," Harlan explained. "Anyway, he promised to accept help from one of us if he needs it. But what about us, Carol? I've missed you every damned day, and I'd like to start seeing you again."

"But Harlan, Kim's education is only the tip of the iceberg," she said. "Fundamentally, we have totally different outlooks on life. I don't understand your easygoing attitude any more than you understand my success-oriented philosophy. And it's not that one of us is right and the other is wrong, it's just that we're so different. Do you really think we have a chance of making a relationship work?"

Harlan thought a minute. "Well, I have to admit we do have some differences, but we share a lot of common ground too. We share Brandon and Kim, a grandchild, the same religion, and sometimes I've been surprised at how much alike our political opinions are. But, more important, Carol, think about all the things we did together while we were dating. Who else do you know who loves a museum as much as you do? Or who's as crazy about going to the movies? And we can talk for hours—I haven't talked this much to a woman since Wanda died. Aren't all those things important? Aren't they more important than the fact that you have a fancy career and I don't?"

"Yes, we've shared all those things and more," Carol said slowly. "But don't you understand? It's not the fact that I have a fancy career, as you put it, and you don't. It's that you don't understand the importance that my career holds for me, or the sacrifices I'm willing to make to pursue it, just like I can't understand how you can play hooky and go fishing in the middle of the week."

"I'll have to try to understand your point of view," Harlan said. "Just like you'll have to try to understand mine. I don't know if we'll make it or not, but don't you think we ought to at least give it a try? I don't want to look back someday and regret that we didn't even make the effort."

"Would you honestly regret it if we didn't try to have something together?" she asked, reaching for his hand.

"Yes, Carol, I would," Harlan admitted. "Come here." He held out his arms and Carol perched on his knee. "I want to start seeing you again very much," he said as he wrapped his arms around her. "Unless you'd prefer Scott."

"No, I wouldn't prefer Scott."

"So what about us?" Harlan asked. "You and me? Will you take me back into your life?"

"Yes, I'll take you back," Carol said, turning in his lap and wrapping her arms around his neck. "I've missed kissing you so much," she said as they met in a sweet, soul-satisfying kiss.

Harlan opened his lips and teased hers into a more intimate, satisfying embrace. She gave herself up to the gentle passion of his loving touch, her own desire flaming. She cradled his nape in her palm, delighting in his strength and the thick, dark hair curling in her fingers.

Harlan peppered quick, passionate kisses all over her face—her lips, her cheeks, her eyelids. "I've missed kissing you, touching you," he said. "I've missed holding you and wanting to protect you."

"Oh, Harlan, I think you're the first man who's ever wanted to protect me," Carol said, tears shimmering in her eyes. "You don't know how wonderful that makes me feel."

She caressed his shoulders and chest through his shirt. She needed him, wanted him more than she could remember wanting any man. She wanted to hold him and have him love her and hold her until morning. She was ready to let him come close to her, to grant him the intimacy she had denied him before. She leaned back and stared into Harlan's eyes. "What are we going to do this time around?"

"You mean about making love? I'll leave that up to you," Harlan said softly. "I want to become your lover, Carol, nothing would make me happier. But I also want you to want it as much as I do. Because once I do make love to you, I won't be able to back off and be just your friend again."

"Neither will I," Carol admitted. She looked into Harlan's eyes and saw tenderness and passion there. "Do you suppose it was like this for Brandon and Kim?" she asked softly. "Is that why they became lovers?"

"I doubt it. They're just kids. I want you the way a man wants a woman, Carol," Harlan said.

"And I want you the way a woman wants a man," she said softly. "Take me to bed," she whispered. "Make love to me until morning."

"My pleasure," Harlan said as he held her in his arms and stood up.

Carol looped her arms around Harlan's neck. "My bedroom's on the end," she said as he started down the darkened hall. Harlan entered her bedroom and put her down beside the bed.

"No," she protested when he reached for the light.

Harlan turned on the small lamp beside the bed instead. "I want some light," he said. "Half the pleasure will be seeing you." He stroked the side of her face.

"Shall I protect us?" Carol asked.

Harlan shook his head. "I had a vasectomy after Wanda's first operation." He reached out and started unbuttoning Carol's blouse. "I've dreamed about you every night."

"You should have come and talked to me," Carol said. "I dreamed about you too."

"Did you dream of making love to me?" Harlan asked as he pushed the blouse off her shoulders.

Carol shook her head slightly. "My dreams weren't that pleasant. I kept dreaming about you walking away from me. I'd call your name and you wouldn't hear me."

"I hear you tonight," Harlan said as he unhooked her bra and drew it from her arms. "Beautiful, just beautiful," he said as he caressed the underside of one of her high, firm breasts.

Carol quickly unbuttoned Harlan's shirt and pushed it off his shoulders. "You don't have the body of a forty-year-old," she said as she ran swift, eager fingers down his chest to the edge of his waistband. Daringly, she unhooked his belt and unzipped his pants. They quickly undressed, but Carol found herself lowering her eyes to the floor.

"Feeling shy?" Harlan asked gently.

Carol nodded. "There have been very few men since my divorce," she admitted. "I'm not used to this at all."

"That's all right, I don't have the longest list in Houston, either," Harlan said candidly. He sat down and pulled her down beside him. "But I don't know why you're shy. You have one of the most appealing bodies I've seen."

Carol ran a self-conscious hand down her abdomen. "My stretch marks never went away," she said softly. "Jack hated them."

"Like I've said, your ex is a real jerk," Harlan said as he pushed her down on the bed. He ran a hand down her soft, silvery-lined stomach. "How any man could hate the marks that gave him a child is beyond me," he said as he dipped his head and ran his tongue around her navel. "I like these marks. They gave me a beautiful daughter-in-law." He kissed one of the lines softly.

"Harlan, you have the most beautiful spirit of any man I've ever known," Carol said as he kissed her stomach gently. Her shyness gone, she raised her head and looked at his naked body stretched across the bed next to hers. Hard and lean, there wasn't the slightest trace of fat anywhere. His back and shoulder muscles were firm, earned day after day at work, and his thighs and calves, sprinkled with the same dark hair that covered his chest, seemed to be carved from stone. Even his bottom was hard and muscular.

"Turn over," Carol said. "I want to see you."

Harlan turned over, letting Carol feast on his masculine perfection. As Carol's eyes traveled downward, past his chest and his waist, a jagged scar on his hip caught her attention.

"See, I'm not perfect either," he said softly. "My souvenir from Nam."

"I didn't know you'd been in the service," Carol said as she touched the scar with gentle fingers. "There's so much about you that I don't know, Harlan."

"There's a lot I don't know about you too, Carol. But just think of how much fun we're going to have learning all those things." He rolled her onto her back and covered her body with his own, meeting her lips in a long, passionate kiss.

Carol reveled in the feeling of Harlan's warm body covering hers. His chest brushed the tips of her breasts and the soft hair on his waist brushed against hers, arousing the passion she had always kept banked. She could feel his arousal and moved to accommodate him, but he shook his head and touched her lower stomach.

"Not yet," he said softly. He stroked her stomach as he dipped his head and caressed the tip of her breast. "I want this to be perfect," he said as he circled her nipple and sucked gently until it was hard. His lips grazed the valley between her breasts before they tormented her other nipple into a knot of desire. "So beautiful," he whispered as his hands stroked her narrow waist.

"You're beautiful too," Carol said as she touched him with desire and passion. Reveling in their newfound freedom, she stroked and caressed him boldly, finding the indention of his waist, the narrowness of his hips, the hardness of his bottom. As Harlan's lips teased their way down her body, past her waist and down her stomach, Carol's touch grew bolder, finding the soft skin at the edge of his hip before touching him intimately, his evident need arousing her even more. She gasped when his lips broke past the barrier of intimacy and caressed her, drawing an involuntary groan from her parted lips. "Oh, Harlan . . ."

"I can't wait any longer," Harlan said as he raised himself up and plunged into her. Carol gasped and instinctively tightened herself around him.

"Oh, sweetheart, you feel so good." Harlan groaned as they began to move together.

Slowly, cautiously at first, they made love, savoring the delight of finally being together and sharing the intimacy they had both wanted for so long. Harlan covered Carol's lips in a long, tender kiss, but as their passion soared even kisses were forgotten as they focused totally on the act of love. Each seemed to know what the other one would like, and the more pleasure they sought to give, the more pleasure came to them. Carol was surprised by her swift ascent to the heights of passion, and as she gasped in awed delight she could hear Harlan groan above her as pleasure overtook him too.

They lay quietly, still together intimately, as their breathing returned to normal.

"Did it kind of sneak up on you too?" Harlan asked. "Are you satisfied?"

Carol nodded. Harlan moved off her and she curled up at his side. "Do you suppose it will always be that fast for us?" she asked.

"I hope not!" Harlan laughed as he stroked her stomach. "Sometimes it would be nice to take it nice and slow."

"Do you have to work tomorrow?" Carol asked. "Should I set the alarm?"

"No, we can sleep in, if you don't mind my car in your driveway," Harlan said.

"Why should I mind?" Carol asked. "I'm proud to be your lover."

Harlan smiled shyly. "I wasn't sure you would be." He put his arm around her. "I wonder what we should do about Brandon and Kim?"

"They knew we were dating before," Carol said. "I don't think we need to tell them everything."

"That's true. They certainly didn't tell us, did they?"

They laughed easily, then Carol turned out the light and snuggled into Harlan's arms. Tonight had been beautiful, a natural step in the relationship that was growing between them, and Carol was glad they had taken that step. But she couldn't help wonder, as she drifted to sleep in his arms, if two people who were so different could really find happiness.

Spent but not sleepy, Harlan pulled Carol closer and sighed as he kissed her hair. She was a beautiful, special lady, and he knew he would always remember the beauty they had found that night. But would they have more than just a brief affair and memories? Harlan knew that what he felt for Carol was different, and he sensed that her feelings for him were much more than casual. He only hoped that would be enough to help them overcome their differences and share the warm, loving relationship he craved.

CHAPTER EIGHT

Carol dragged herself into the house and tossed her briefcase on her desk. If she had any sense, she would have left the bulging briefcase at the office, or at least in the car, but she thought she might get a little of her paperwork done that evening before Harlan came. He had offered to take her out for a simple supper before they got the next day's Thanksgiving dinner started for the two of them and the kids. Carol appreciated Harlan's offer to help, especially since he wasn't really in his element in the kitchen, but she almost wished he weren't coming tonight. She was tired and irritable, and Harlan knew her well enough by now to see through her social facade. He would want to know what was wrong, and Carol hated telling him that it was tension at work that was making her unhappy, since she knew he wouldn't understand.

Carol made herself a cup of herbal tea and sat down in the comfortable chair beside her bed, glancing around the room where she and Harlan had spent so many happy hours recently. Harlan's car had become a familiar sight in her driveway, appearing most evenings at least for a little while and sometimes staying until morning. Their affair had been passionate and fulfilling, and Carol found herself happier than she had been in years. Harlan was kind, and tender, and funny, and she was beginning to hope that maybe, just maybe they could someday make their relationship permanent.

But their affair was far from idyllic. They were both trying very hard to understand one another's point of view concerning careers or, more specifically, Carol's career. Carol knew he disapproved of the toll it took on her, but she honestly couldn't see any alternative if she expected to continue to do well in it. She wondered how much longer Harlan would say nothing to her about his disapproval, and what she would say when he did choose to comment. She didn't want to argue with him, but she also felt that her job was her business, and hoped that Harlan would understand that.

Carol showered and put on a pair of comfortable jeans. As she zipped the waistband, she noticed that the pants were somewhat looser than they had been when she bought them in the summer. Shrugging, she put on a blouse and dabbed on some concealer under her eyes and a little blusher before sitting down to do some of the paperwork she had brought home with her. Unfortunately, the paperwork was just as irritating to her as her day at work had been, and her mood wasn't the best in the world when Harlan rang the doorbell.

Carol hurried to the door and lifted her face for his kiss. "You're a sight for sore eyes," she said as he enveloped her in a warm embrace.

Harlan kissed her gently and held her to him. "You look tired," he said tenderly. "Long day?"

"And it's still not over," Carol said as she shut the door behind them. "There's a kitchen full of things to do tonight."

"Carol, we could always take the kids out tomorrow," Harlan said. "There are plenty of restaurants that will be serving turkey. The kids would understand."

Carol squeezed his hand. "I know, but I don't mind fixing dinner. I find it kind of relaxing, in fact."

"Well, if you're sure," Harlan said. He glanced toward the living room. When he spotted the pile of papers on her desk, his lips thinned a little. She had been working on that damned job of hers again when she should have put it from her mind until Friday. "Where would you like to eat?"

"Somewhere they have good, old-fashioned cooking," Carol said. "Just a minute and I'll be ready."

Harlan followed Carol out to the kitchen where she got a pill out of the bottle on the counter.

"Is that one of your stomach pills?" he asked. "You don't usually take one until nine or ten."

Carol took a breath and swallowed the pill. "I know, but if I want to keep anything down, I need the pill tonight." She drank a little water to wash it down. "I didn't realize you knew when I take my medication."

Harlan smiled slightly. "It's amazing how much I've learned about you in the last few weeks," he said. "I've learned that you sleep curled up in a ball, that you make the best French toast in the world, that you hog the water in the shower—"

"I do not hog the water!" Carol said indignantly.

"A matter of opinion." Harlan grinned. "But I've also learned that you work too hard, Carol," he said as he reached out and touched the circle under her eye. "You think I don't know what's underneath the makeup?"

"Should I start wearing makeup to bed?" Carol asked dryly.

"No," Harlan said. "I don't need a mouthful of lipstick when I kiss you. But I'm worried about you, Carol."

"I'm fine," she said shortly. "Why don't we go to Aunt Esther's Goodies? They have the best fried chicken this side of Houston."

"Sounds great." When they got outside Harlan opened the car door for her. "But you're not changing the subject, Carol," he said as he backed out of her driveway. "I am worried about you."

"Harlan, I'm fine," she said. "I'm just tired from work. We had a rush of investing this week, I don't know why, and the telephone rang off the hook. I got nothing done at my desk, as I usually do, and I've had to carry it home with me for the last three nights."

"Which means that you worked on it after I left at eleven on Monday," Harlan said. "You should have said something! I would have left sooner."

Carol stroked his thigh. "But I didn't want you to leave. And I only worked for an hour or so that night."

"And last night?"

"Well, quite a while. But that's just part of the job. If I'm going to continue to do well in it, I have to put in that kind of effort."

Harlan pulled out a pack of cigarettes and offered her one. "Have you ever thought that maybe, just maybe, this job's too much for a woman? Now I know—"

"How can you say such a thing?" Carol protested angrily. "Too much for a woman? Good grief, do you realize how chauvinistic that sounds? Women today are going into all professions—medicine, law, business—"

"That isn't what I meant," Harlan said impatiently. "And I'm not a chauvinist. What I was trying to say was that maybe that job would be too much for a man as well as a woman. Maybe most men couldn't handle it, either. I doubt I could."

"But Harlan, any job that's financially rewarding is either physically or mentally gruelling," Carol argued. "You ought to know that. You're exhausted by the end of the day."

"I'm not all that worn out!" Harlan protested.

"Then why did you fall asleep on the couch last Monday night in the middle of a football game?" Carol asked smugly. "One that you'd been looking forward to for a week?"

"All right, I get physically tired," Harlan said. "But I'm not tense and wound up like a spring. I don't come home from work and have to take a stomach pill because I'm tied up in knots. And I'm not smoking too much, like you are. Look, I know you think I'm interfering and that I'm way out of line for even bringing it up, but the pace you keep and all the stress isn't good for you."

"Harlan, please don't worry about me," Carol said tightly. "I'm fine, honestly. And please let's not argue any more. If we do I sure won't be able to eat."

"All right." Harlan clearly wasn't pleased, but he said no

more. He pulled into the parking lot of the restaurant and took her by the shoulders. "Let me get your mind off everything."

"Harlan, people are looking," Carol protested, but he pulled her close and covered her lips in a long, passionate kiss that left her senses reeling. When he finally released her, Carol's cheeks were flushed with passion and embarrassment. "Those kids saw everything!" she whispered.

"Good. I hope they learned a thing or two," Harlan said, winking at the gawking young couple in the next car. "Do you feel better?"

"A lot," Carol admitted. She ate a huge supper, the first decent meal she had eaten all day, and she and Harlan spent the evening laughing and talking as he chopped vegetables for the dressing and she made a pecan pie. Harlan did not bring up the subject of her job and neither did she. But Carol knew that they had not solved their difference of opinion. They had merely temporarily shelved the issue.

Harlan accepted Carol's invitation to stay the night. As always, their lovemaking was special, and Carol was exhausted and satisfied as she snuggled into Harlan's arms. But she lay awake staring into the darkness long after Harlan's even breathing told her he was asleep. Although that night's argument had not been all that serious, it did leave her worried about their relationship. Apparently Harlan was no closer to accepting her involvement with her job or the effect the pressure and strain had on her than he ever had been. And there was no way that any kind of permanent relationship between them would work until he was able to do that.

"Oh, hell, it would ring when my hands are full," Carol grumbled as she fumbled with the roasting pan. "Coming!" she called, wondering whether it was Harlan or the kids.

She ran to the door and Harlan pulled her into his arms for a tender kiss. "Do we have time before the kids get here?" he asked.

"After last night and this morning, I'd think you'd be worn out," Carol teased.

"You would think that, but you just have this effect on me," Harlan said, smiling. He smelled of soap and aftershave, and Carol wished they really did have time before the kids were due to arrive. "How's dinner coming along?"

"Just fine," Carol assured him. "Did you bring your satchel?"

"I left it in the car until after Kim and Brandon leave," Harlan said dryly. "No sense in advertising."

Carol raised her eyebrows. "I'm surprised they haven't caught on by now. We haven't exactly made a secret of it."

"Oh, they're off in their own little world," he said breezily. "Those two kids are so much in love I don't think they would know or care if we made love in front of them."

"I guess not," Carol replied. At that moment the sports car pulled into the driveway and shuddered to a halt. Brandon got out and marched to the house, obviously trying to control his anger. Kim got out and slammed her door.

"What was that about being in love?" Carol asked dryly.

Harlan put his hand on Carol's shoulder. "Whatever it is this time, let's stay out of it."

Carol nodded, hoping Brandon wasn't trying to get Kim to drop out of school again. Both of the young people had their expressions mostly under control by the time they reached the front porch.

"Kim, Brandon, it's good to see you," Carol said warmly, successfully masking her concern. "Harlan just beat you here."

"Thanks for having us," Brandon said. "Everything smells delicious."

"I've looked forward to this all week," Kim said as she hugged her mother. Carol thought she could see the sheen of tears in Kim's eyes, and longed to know what had the girl so upset, but she had promised to stay out of this fight, whatever it was about.

Harlan mixed himself and Brandon a drink. Kim offered to

help in the kitchen, but she looked so tired Harlan insisted that she sit down, and he and Carol put the finishing touches on dinner. Carol wondered if either Kim or Brandon noticed the ease with which Harlan worked in the kitchen, or the fact that he knew where everything was, but they were too absorbed in their own argument, whatever it was, to notice or care.

Carol's dinner was delicious, but the atmosphere between Kim and Brandon was strained, leaving Carol and Harlan to do most of the talking. They asked Kim about finals coming up and talked with Brandon about the additional crew he had taken on last week, giving Harlan more time to do his paperwork, but neither of them did much more than respond to direct questions. Harlan and Carol finally gave up, and Kim and Brandon spent the rest of dinner glowering at each other across the table.

"What gives with those two?" Harlan whispered as he and Carol carried dinner plates into the kitchen.

Carol glanced back into the dining room. "Do you want me to try to find out?" she asked quietly.

"I think we'd be better off if we stayed out of it," he said. "If they're squabbling about her going to school, we'll just end up mad at each other again."

"He better not—"

Harlan put his finger to Carol's lips. "See what I mean?" he asked. "But I don't think it's that."

"Maybe it's something really trivial," Carol said. "I hope it is."

They cut slices of pie and carried them out to the dining room. Carol brought out the coffee and poured a cup for everyone.

"Well, Brandon, are you ready for the hunting trip next week?" Harlan asked as he cut into his pie.

"Yes, Brandon, are you ready for the hunting trip?" Kim sneered across the table.

Carol almost dropped her fork. She had never heard Kim use

that tone of voice with Brandon—or anyone else, for that matter.

"Yes, I'm ready," Brandon said grimly. "And I'm going, whether you like it or not, Kimberly."

"Damn you, Brandon Stone, I asked you to stay home next weekend!" Kim said as she threw her napkin onto the table. She burst into tears and jumped up, running into the family room and sitting down on the couch.

Brandon threw his napkin down. "She's being totally unreasonable about this!" he snapped. "One weekend! One lousy weekend, and she's having a fit!" He got up and followed his wife.

Harlan looked irritated and impatient. "What's with her?" he grumbled.

Carol shook her head sadly. "I thought she'd forgotten about that," she said, more to herself than to Harlan. "I'll go talk to her."

Completely mystified, Harlan followed Carol into the family room. Carol sat down on the couch and put her arm around Kim.

"Kim, honey, it's all right," she soothed. "Get yourself together and let's talk about this." She glanced up at her son-in-law. "Sit down, Brandon."

Brandon eyed Carol warily and sat down. "It's not like I'm going to West Texas or something," he began defensively. "If she goes into labor I can be there in forty-five minutes or less and—"

"Brandon, this doesn't have a thing to do with you," Carol said.

"Yes, it does!" Kim said, her eyes filling with fresh tears. "He's got someone else, I just know it. I'm big and ugly and I can't make love any more, and he's found another woman!"

Carol started laughing and crying at the same time. "No, he hasn't, Kim," she said, glancing from Harlan to Brandon. "Now you sit up, stop crying, and listen to me. Harlan told me about this hunting trip a week or so ago. He and Brandon take all the trimmers to a little cabin they rent, and they play cards and go to bed early and they really do go hunting. It's not like it was with your father, Kim." Carol looked up and blushed painfully. "That used to be Jack's standard excuse when he wanted to take a girlfriend out of town for the weekend."

"Oh," Brandon said.

"Kim, surely you don't think Brandon's seeing someone else," Carol said gently. "I've never seen a young man as crazy about his wife as he is about you. Besides, when would he have time? He works all day and then he goes straight home to you, doesn't he?"

"Aw, Kim, I wouldn't do that to you!" Brandon said as he sat down beside her. "I love you too much. You're my wife, you're having my baby—I would no more cheat on you than—than—"

"He wouldn't, Kim," Harlan said gently, kneeling in front of Kim. "He does love you very much, and he believes in marriage the same way I do. I never cheated on his mother."

"Lucky woman," Carol murmured.

"Besides, Kim, you're the only one I ever—uh, you know!" Brandon said, blushing brightly.

Carol and Harlan looked at each other and fought not to laugh. "Kim, you have every reason to trust Brandon," she said quietly.

Kim looked into Brandon's eyes. "I'm sorry," she said as more tears rolled down her cheeks. "I was just so scared!"

"It's all right, honey," Brandon said. He put his arms around Kim and kissed her cheeks. "I love you and I'm not going to cheat on you."

Harlan looked down at Carol's bent head and felt a surge of love and affection for her. It had embarrassed her to admit that her husband had cheated on her, and he had not missed her murmured comment about his own marriage. But she hadn't let it sour her toward all men, and she had eloquently expressed her faith in the son he had raised. He put his hand on Carol's head. "Thanks," he said quietly.

"You're welcome," she said, tears shimmering in her eyes.

Harlan handed Kim his handkerchief. "Now that the hunting trip's settled, could we finish Carol's pie? The one bite I had was delicious."

"Let's not go back to the table," Carol suggested. "I'll bring the pie in here."

Harlan and Carol carried in the pie and Brandon brought the coffee pot and fresh cups. They enjoyed Carol's pie, and Kimberly insisted on helping to clean up. "It's the least I can do after upsetting everybody," she said as she took Brandon's empty plate.

"Don't worry about upsetting everybody," Carol said. "It's better to have that kind of thing out in the open. Now that you know it really is just a hunting trip you can stop worrying. But I would feel better if you stayed over here that weekend."

"I second that," Harlan said as he came through with another handful of dishes. "You're getting pretty big."

"Thanks," Kim said dryly as she reached around and rubbed the small of her back.

Carol eyed her daughter's figure. "Kim, I swear you look like you've dropped. What did the doctor say yesterday?"

"She said I wasn't anywhere near having the baby and that I could go back to school Monday with no problem," Kim said cheerfully. She bumped the front of the counter. "This kitchen's smaller than it used to be."

With Kim's clumsy help, Carol managed to get the mess cleaned up, and she and Brandon left a little while later. Carol collapsed onto the couch and lit a cigarette. "I should have taken you up on your offer of a restaurant meal," she said as Harlan sat down beside her. "That's a lot of work!"

"But it was delicious," Harlan said as he took Carol's hand. "I appreciate more than the dinner, you know. Thank you for your faith in Brandon. That meant a lot to me. I know he wasn't exactly the husband you wanted for her."

"I've come to the conclusion that Kim knows more about picking husbands than I did," Carol said thoughtfully.

"Brandon's a good man—he's generous and faithful. That means a lot, Harlan."

"Is it that big a deal, being faithful?" Harlan asked. "Is it all that hard to manage?"

"For some people it is," Carol said. "Jack cheated on me off and on during our entire marriage. I created a stink every time I found out, but it seldom did any good. Oh, he'd usually break it off, but he was at it again in a matter of months. Kim saw all that, Harlan, which was why she came unglued about the hunting trip. She may have a harder time trusting Brandon than a lot of girls would, and that's a shame, because he's one man who deserves to be trusted. I hope she and Brandon will talk about it some more tonight."

"What about you?" Harlan asked gently. "How did Jack's unfaithfulness affect you? It doesn't seem to have left you bitter against men or anything like that."

"Well, no, it wouldn't do that," Carol said. "I grew up in a happy home, and Dad never cheated on Mama, so I knew that not all men were like Jack. But it didn't do wonders for my self-esteem. I kept thinking, 'Why can't I satisfy him? Why can't I hold him?' I kept searching for my inadequacy. I guess deep down I still wonder if there was something lacking in me that made him seek other women for satisfaction."

"Carol, there's no way that his infidelity was your fault," he assured her. "You're the most wonderful lover a man could ask for, so if there was anything lacking, it was on his part, not yours. You could keep a man satisfied forever."

Carol turned to Harlan, and he was surprised to see tears shimmering in her eyes. "Do you mean that?" she asked. "I've always wondered."

"You mean none of the men since have told you?" Harlan asked. "Carol, you're a terrific, beautiful lover. You excite me like no other woman ever has." He ran his hand down the side of her face. "I could never cheat on you," he said as he leaned forward and touched her lips gently with his own.

Carol's lips softened against his, responding with the same

gentleness as they caressed one another tenderly. "Thank you," she whispered against his lips before she leaned forward, increasing the pressure of their embrace. Harlan cradled her head between his palms, weaving his fingers through her shimmering locks and softly massaging her scalp. Every touch of Harlan's conveyed love, and caring, and tenderness, and Carol opened to his affection like a rose blooming in the spring.

"I love you," Harlan said hesitantly as he met her eyes shyly. "I know I'm not the kind of man you—"

"And I'm not the kind of woman, either, am I?" Carol asked softly. "But I'm not surprised. I love you too, Harlan. I've loved you for quite a while now."

"You do?" Harlan asked. "Oh, Carol, I was hoping you'd say that," he confessed as he pulled her to him, his arms wrapping around her waist.

"I've never experienced the kind of caring and tenderness with another man that I have with you." She held him close and stroked his back.

Harlan leaned back and looked down at her. "Would you like to celebrate?"

Carol nodded. "Get your bag."

She was turning back the bed when Harlan came in the bedroom. "Would you mind waiting while I shower?" she asked. "I smell like eau de turkey."

"Fine," Harlan said easily. Carol ducked into the bathroom and had just gotten into the shower when Harlan, as naked as she, joined her. "I thought you might need your back scrubbed," he said as he turned her around. "My, what a view!"

Together they stared into the full-length mirror placed just outside the shower stall. Harlan was standing to the side of her, and Carol marveled at the mature sensuality of their naked bodies. They were both tall and slim, and Harlan's toughly muscled body was a perfect foil for her feminine curves.

Harlan reached up and caressed her breast, and the tip immediately grew hard. "I love to see you do that," he said, wrapping his arms around her. He cradled her other breast and caressed it too.

Harlan caressed the front of her body before he picked up a bar of soap and lovingly soaped her breasts and her waist, every stroke inflaming her. Her breath started coming in uneven little gasps, the most telling outward sign of her growing excitement. Harlan's desire was growing more evident too in the steaming confines of the shower. He loved her and he needed her, and Carol reveled in the knowledge.

Harlan thoroughly caressed her front before he pushed her away just a little. "Beautiful," he said as he nibbled her nape before soaping the tender skin there. Carol shivered as he made his way down her back and sides, his touch growing more teasing and erotic the closer he came to her soft bottom. He teased and caressed her there, drawing pictures with his fingers and making Carol laugh. "Beats a tablet!" he said when Carol protested.

"Harlan, that's enough!" Carol exclaimed as she turned around. She picked up another bar of soap and started to wash Harlan just as he had washed her. She felt him grow taut with desire as she caressed his body with her slick fingers, teasing him and drawing the strength and passion from him.

"God, how I love you," Harlan said as he pressed her against the cool tile and opened her lips for a searing kiss. She responded instantly, burying her fingers in his hair and pressing her naked body closer to his. She could feel every inch of his hard, masculine warmth trapping her against the wall, and she gloried in the strength of his desire for her.

"I want you," he murmured as he started to nudge her legs apart.

"Not in here, we'll break our necks," Carol protested. Her fingers trembling with need, she turned off the shower and they quickly grabbed towels. Before Carol could dry herself completely, Harlan whisked her off her feet and carried her to the bed.

"I love you, Harlan," she said as she pulled him down with her. "Make love to me, please."

Harlan deftly rolled her on top of him. "Make love to me," he commanded her hoarsely. "Show me your love, Carol."

Carol smiled wickedly and did something she had never done with Harlan before. With loving caresses, she proceeded to love him all over, then shifted her body so that they were together. Harlan moaned and cried out her name, and she could feel his strength pouring into her.

It took Harlan a few minutes for his breathing to return to normal. "That was beautiful," he said. "But you didn't let me give you satisfaction."

"That was my gift to you," Carol said gently as she eased herself off him.

Harlan pushed her down into the sheets. "Then by all means, let me return the gift," he said as his lips and hands wandered down her body, touching and caressing her in the ways she loved so much. He teased and touched her breasts, made his way inch by loving inch to her stomach, and finally crossed the barrier to love her intimately. Carol relaxed and gave herself up to the pleasure of his touch, every kiss and caress a testament of his love. Her passion soared quickly, but not so quickly that she couldn't savor the piercing sweetness of his embrace. She wanted it to end, she wanted it to go on forever, she wanted the passion to come and never go away. When the delight finally did come, she gasped and quivered at the cascades of pleasure that broke over her, wave after wave shaking her slender frame.

"Oh, Harlan, I—what are you doing?" she asked as Harlan lifted himself over her.

"I need you again, Carol," he said as he joined their bodies together. Carol could only marvel at the strength of their passion as they soared once more. Their bodies finely tuned to each other's needs, they rocked together, slowly reaching for the second pinnacle, and finally cried out once again.

Harlan rolled off Carol and lay back, exhausted. "I thought that kind of loving was over years ago."

"I didn't realize it even existed," Carol admitted as she snuggled beside him.

"I love you." He kissed her cheek tenderly.

"I love you too," Carol murmured. "Are you asleep yet?"

"No, actually I'm hungry again," Harlan said.

"I can't believe it." Carol laughed. "No, on second thought, I could use another piece of that pie too." She climbed out of bed and pulled on her robe. "Stay put. I'll bring it in here."

Harlan sighed as he watched Carol glide out of the bedroom. She looked happy that night, happier than she ever had, and he was gratified to know that he had made her look that way by loving her and telling her so. But did their love have a chance, with everything else they had going against them? Would their love be enough to carry them through?

Carol lifted her head and squinted at the alarm clock, which read five-twelve. "What's that godawful ringing?" she mumbled. She fumbled for the telephone but heard only the dial tone.

Harlan raised himself up on one elbow. "I think it's the doorbell." He yawned.

Carol instantly stiffened. "What could anybody be doing out there at this hour of the morning?"

"I don't know, but I'll go down," Harlan said. He slid out of bed and pulled on his slacks as Carol tied on her terry-cloth robe.

They hurried to the front of the house and jerked open the door just as the bell rang again. "Dad!" Brandon said, horrified. "What are you doing here?"

"I was sound asleep until just a minute ago," Harlan said dryly.

"I mean, what are you doing sleeping at Carol's house?"

Carol blushed furiously as Kim pushed herself out of the car. "What's going—Harlan, what are you still doing here?"

Brandon turned around to Kimberly. "My God, my father's sleeping with your mother!"

"Oh, no!" Kimberly said as her hand flew to her mouth. "Mother, how could you?"

"The same way you could, only I have enough sense not to end up like you did," Carol said dryly.

"But Dad, aren't you a little old for this?" Brandon asked, utterly shocked.

Carol laughed before she could help herself. "Hardly. Believe me, your father's a long way from being too old."

"Brand, you're in no position to pass judgment on my sex life," Harlan said, biting his lip to keep from laughing. "What on earth are you doing out at this hour? Kim's not in labor, is she?"

"Yes, I am, and I wanted Mother to come along," Kim said. A contraction overcame her and she winced, suddenly looking young and frightened.

"Give me five minutes," Carol said, running toward her room to dress.

"Ditto," Harlan said, following her down the hall.

Brandon turned to Kim. "I knew they went out sometimes, but I sure didn't know it had gone this far."

Kim rolled her eyes. "I didn't even think she liked him that much. What's gotten into them?"

Brandon thought a minute. "I think they must be having their midlife crises. That's all it could be."

Harlan and Carol followed Kim and Brandon to the hospital, laughing all the way at their children's horror when they realized what was going on.

"Do you think they'll ever get over the shock?" Harlan asked, his eyes twinkling.

"I think that by the end of the day they'll have a whole lot more to worry about than our love life," Carol said confidently. They parked and Carol waited with Kimberly while Brandon filled out the admission forms. Although Kim didn't seem to be in that much pain yet, she was frightened in spite of her childbirth training, and Carol didn't envy the girl the next few hours.

Kim and Brandon disappeared into a labor room, and Carol and Harlan settled down in the waiting room.

The morning passed slowly. They let Carol in to see Kim a couple of times, and she found her daughter less frightened than she had seemed earlier. Harlan brought them coffee and doughnuts from the cafeteria, and Carol spelled Brandon for a few minutes so he could eat. Carol tried to get interested in a magazine, and then in the portable television that was mounted on the wall, but every few minutes her eyes would creep to the clock and over to the double doors that separated her from Kim.

"I hate this waiting!" she snapped in frustration. "It's almost easier to have the baby yourself."

"I think I'll pass on that one," Harlan said dryly.

Brandon slammed open the double door a few minutes before noon, a huge grin on his face. "Heather Eileen says to tell Grandma and Grandad hi," he said proudly.

"Oh, it's a girl!" Carol cried. "Is she all right? How big is she? How's Kim?"

"The baby and Kim are fine, and Heather weighs seven and a half pounds," he said. "They're supposed to bring the crib to the door so you can get a better look."

Just then, a smiling nurse wheeled a portable incubator up to the door. "Come meet your granddaughter," she said softly.

Carol and Harlan bent over the crib and stared at the tiny infant, hastily wrapped in a hospital blanket. She was alert, but she wasn't crying—she was flailing her fists and looking around with surprisingly sharp eyes.

"Oh, she's beautiful," Carol breathed as tears clouded her eyes. "Harlan, did you ever see such a beautiful child?"

"Once," he said as he stared down at the little girl. Tears ran down his face and he made no effort to hide them. "Brandon, you and Kim have a beautiful child," he said.

"You folks can see her some more in a little while," the nurse said. "We need to wash her up now."

"Can I come?" Brandon asked eagerly.

"You can watch from the glass windows. You and your wife can have the baby tonight for as long as you want."

Brandon completely forgot Carol and Harlan and followed the nurse.

Carol turned to Harlan and wiped the tears from his cheeks. "Oh, Harlan, she's so precious!" she said happily. "We have a grandchild!"

Harlan picked her up and whirled her around. "Yes, we do, don't we? We have the most wonderful grandchild in the whole world!"

CHAPTER NINE

Harlan and Carol peered into the glass window of the nursery.

"She looks like Kim," Carol said as she peered at Heather. The baby had been cleaned up and was sleeping peacefully in the isolette.

"No, she looks like Brandon did," Harlan said. "Look here." He whipped out his wallet and pulled out a dog-eared picture of a smiling young woman and a baby. "See?"

Carol looked at the picture a moment and then got out her own wallet. She silently handed Harlan a picture of Kimberly as an infant. "She looks a lot like both of them," she said as Harlan studied the picture. She looked down again at Brandon and his mother. "Wanda was pretty."

"Thank you."

Carol gave him back his picture and put Kimberly's away. They stared at Heather for a few more minutes before Harlan put his arm around Carol's shoulders and led her from the window.

"I don't know about you, but I think I could stand a few hours away from here. We can come back tonight."

They were silent on the way to the car, each lost in his own thoughts. "Tired?" Harlan asked as he backed out of the parking space.

"Not really. How about you?"

"I could use a nap," Harlan admitted. "Care to take one together?"

"I would, but I have to go in and pick up the work I missed

today," Carol admitted. "I had one of the other brokers cover for me, but that leaves me with a lot to do over the weekend. I'll probably go in for a little while Sunday."

They rode for a few minutes in silence. "I feel old," Harlan said suddenly. "I'm a grandfather, for crying out loud!"

"So do I." She sighed. "Knowing you're old enough to be a grandmother's one thing, but actually being one's another story."

"Sweetheart, you're just old enough to be a grandmother," Harlan comforted her. "Hell, for that matter, you're young enough to have another one of your own, if you wanted to."

Carol could not disguise the horror on her face. "You have to be kidding!"

He laughed. "Of course I'm kidding. And we're not all that old, really. We just feel that way."

Carol sighed and slipped on a pair of sunglasses. "I know I'm not all that old, but I sure feel old sometimes. Shoot, when did I ever get to be young, anyway? I was married and a mother by the time I was nineteen. And Jack and I sure as hell didn't have fun together."

"So what about now?" Harlan asked. "I get to do a lot of fun things."

"When do I have time for fun now?" Carol asked. "The only fun I have is with you."

"I take that as a high compliment," Harlan said. "But you'd have more time for fun if your job didn't keep you so busy. There are other jobs—"

"None of which pay as well as stockbroking does," Carol finished neatly. "It's the nature of the job."

"Did you realize that when you started with Purcell-Smith?"

"Of course," she lied glibly. "What did your mother say when you called her?"

Harlan answered Carol politely, determined not to show that he was put out by her reply. It was wrong for her not to have time for fun in her life. It was no wonder she felt old if the only fun she had was the time she spent with him. He drove past a billboard with the Astroworld logo on it and smiled wickedly to himself. Carol didn't know it, but she was going to have a day of fun sooner than she expected.

After reading the letter on the top of the stack, Carol penciled a reply for the secretary to type in the morning. It was Sunday, and the office was very quiet, with the squawk boxes off, the desks empty, and the computer consoles dark. In a way Carol enjoyed the peace, but it did seem strange without the bustle of the usual weekday activity. She read a few more letters and answered them, and was about to check through her Rolodex when she heard the outer door open and the sound of heavy footsteps on the thin carpet. Carol froze. She had let herself in the office building with her key, and as far as she knew, the security guard was down in the lobby—surely he would have called out if it were he. She sat quietly, hoping the intruder wouldn't notice that the light over her desk was on.

Carol gulped as the footsteps came right to her door. She stood and gripped the paperweight from her desk, then held her breath as the door was pushed open.

"Carol—what the *hell?*" Harlan cried as the paperweight flew through the air and missed his head by an inch.

"Harlan! You scared me half to death!" Carol exclaimed as she collapsed into her chair.

"You didn't do me any good, either!" he said as he picked up her makeshift weapon and set it on the desk. "You weren't the pitcher, I assume."

"No, I played first base," Carol replied. "How did you get in?"

"I sweet-talked the security guard," Harlan admitted cheerfully. He placed his hands on Carol's shoulders and kissed her soundly.

"What are you doing here?"

"I've come to kidnap you," he said as he pulled her to her feet. "We're going to have some of that fun you've missed out on."

"Harlan, don't be silly." She put her arms around his neck. "Why did you come, really?"

"I just told you," he replied. "Where's your purse?"

"My wallet's in my pocket," Carol said. "Hey, what are you doing?" she asked as he took her hand and started to lead her out of her office.

"I told you—I'm kidnapping you. We're going to have fun this afternoon."

"But Harlan, I have work to do. I can't go off with you this afternoon!"

"Don't be ridiculous. Of course you can," he said firmly. "You worked at home all day yesterday and you'll work all day tomorrow and every day next week. You owe yourself some time and I'm here to see that you take it."

"Harlan, I really have things to do. I just don't have time to go—"

Harlan silenced her with a long, passionate kiss. "Yes, you do have time," he said with exasperation. "And you're going to have some fun this afternoon one way or the other. Now, do I kidnap you or do I make love to you on your office carpet?" he asked. "Your choice."

She couldn't miss the gleam in his eyes. "You'd do it, wouldn't you?"

"In a flash. Astroworld? Or do I strip you and ravish you right here?"

Carol sighed before she started laughing. "I guess we better go to Astroworld. I don't want the security man walking in on us here."

Harlan waited while she locked her office. "Since when is Astroworld open after Thanksgiving?" she asked as they walked down to Harlan's car.

"They're going to try it for a couple of Sundays and see if they draw enough of a crowd," Harlan said. "Have you been recently?"

"I haven't been since Kim got old enough to start going with her friends," Carol admitted. "How about you?"

"I haven't been in a long time, either."

Harlan drove out to the park and they waited patiently in line between a group of giggling teenagers and a young couple with two small children. Carol felt a little silly, but why shouldn't she and Harlan enjoy a theme park? Harlan took her hand and together they walked into the park. The wind was a little cool, and Harlan had thoughtfully brought her a windbreaker to wear over her blouse. "What do you want to do first?" Harlan asked indulgently.

"All I've heard about for the last two years is something called Thunder River," she answered. "I'd like to go there first."

"Thunder River it is." Harlan bought a map and they made their way through the crowd to the newest and most exciting ride in the park.

"Wow, they're really coming out of there wet," Carol said as a laughing family came out the turnstiles.

"You don't melt, do you?" Harlan teased.

The ride was every bit as exciting as it promised to be. Carol laughed and squealed as they bounced over man-made rapids, the round raft slamming into rocks and splashing them thoroughly.

"Want to do that again?" Harlan teased as he dried her face with a handkerchief.

"Maybe later," Carol said.

They dried off while they waited at the Bamboo Shoot, and promptly got wet again when the "bamboo shoot" they were riding in splashed against the trough. Harlan insisted that the next ride be a dry one, and Carol persuaded him that she simply had to ride the XLR8, a roller coaster–like ride that had the cars suspended from a narrow track high above the ground.

"Are you sure you want to do this?" he asked doubtfully as they climbed into the car.

"Sure, it will be fun," Carol insisted. She squirmed impatiently waiting for the car to start and gasped when it suddenly lurched and began its long, tortuous ascent. "It'll be fun, honestly it will," Carol said, more to herself than to Harlan.

The car broke free of the chain and Carol screamed in terror as the tiny car careened down the track and around a corner.

"Oh, no!" she cried as the car flew up at a sharp angle. "Harlan, get me off this thing!"

"This wasn't my idea!" he yelled as Carol clutched his arm tightly. She buried her head in his chest, quaking with fear as the little car swung around more turns and started up on another conveyor belt.

Carol raised her head and swore. "My God, we're going up for the high one!" She gulped as she buried her head in Harlan's chest again.

Harlan's eyes watered against the wind generated by the car's breathstopping descent. It flew around curves and made one small loop that had them out at almost a ninety-degree angle.

"Oh, get me *off!*" Carol moaned as the car came in for another series of dips.

Carol waited until the car had completely stopped before she lifted her head. "Why didn't you stop me?" she asked hoarsely.

"I've always wanted to date a green woman," Harlan said graciously. "You turn the most appealing shade of lime."

"Oh, shut up." She climbed out of the car as fast as her wobbly legs could carry her.

They spent the rest of the afternoon at the park. They rode all the tamer rides, and Carol worked up her courage to try a few of the rougher ones, finding them tame after the XLR8. She was enchanted by the little European village, created to resemble an Alpine resort, and they were both impressed by the quality of the musical production put on by local college students in the theater. The antique taxis were Carol's favorite ride, and Harlan patiently rode them with her three times. Carol was taken with the delicate creations of glass in the glassblowing shop, and Harlan had the glassblower make her an exquisite bird as a souvenir of their day together.

It was dusk when they finally left the park. Carol had to

admit that she hadn't had that much fun in a long time, and she doubted that Harlan had, either.

"Do you want to go by the hospital and see Heather?" he asked as they got in the car.

"I went by for a few minutes this morning, and I'm going by the apartment tomorrow after work. I hate those hospital rules that keep us from holding her!"

"What are you going to do when she spits up on your fancy business suit?" Harlan teased.

"Are you kidding? I already have clothes in the car. Speaking of which, I need to pick it up."

"Why don't I drop you off in the morning? Is it safe in the lot?"

"Yes, it's safe," Carol said.

Harlan suggested they pick up Chinese food for supper. He grew quiet on the way home, and Carol sensed that something was on his mind. She wondered if he still felt old at the thought of being a grandparent, but didn't think that was what was troubling him. They stopped to get the Chinese food and Carol set out the plates once they were in her kitchen.

"Is something bothering you?" she asked gently as she put her arms around him.

"Not exactly," he said thoughtfully. "Carol, will you marry me?"

Carol took a deep breath and expelled it slowly. "Can we talk about it after we eat?"

"Sure." Harlan opened the containers while she made tea. They ate their food in silence and carried their tea out to the family room, where they sat together on the sofa. "Carol, I love you and I want to spend my life with you," Harlan said as he took her hand in his. "We have something that I thought I'd never find again after Wanda died. And I know that you love me."

"But is that enough?" Carol asked quietly. "Yes, we love each other like I've never loved before, but we have some differences, some really big differences, that won't go away."

"You mean because I'm not a professional man?" Harlan asked a little bitterly. "Am I not fancy enough to introduce at the office?"

"Harlan, that's not what I meant at all!" she said with exasperation. "And as far as I'm concerned, I could introduce you to anyone anywhere. It's a difference in values, Harlan. You couldn't understand why Kim and I wanted her to stay in school, and you don't understand the time and energy I put into my work."

"I understand about Kim now, and I'm trying to understand about the stockbroking," Harlan argued. "I really am trying my best. But those aren't such big differences when you look at all the things we do have in common. I'm just not willing to pass up what we could share, Carol. We could have such a wonderful life together."

"I'm just not sure," Carol said as she bit her lip. "Do you honestly think we could make a marriage work? I've had one marriage go bad on me, and I couldn't deal with another disaster."

"It won't be a disaster, Carol, honestly," Harlan said. "Will you at least let me give you an engagement ring for Christmas? I'm not going to push you into a hasty wedding until you're sure that marrying me is what you want."

"Oh, Harlan, I'm sure it's what I want, I'm just not sure it will work," Carol admitted as she threw herself into his arms.

Harlan lowered his head and met her mouth in a long, searing kiss. "Take my ring," he said. "Please."

Carol nodded, too overcome with love to refuse him anything. Harlan kissed her deeply as his fingers worked magic on her body, persuading her with love and passion to become his wife. He touched her and caressed her, and gradually their clothes came off in a heap next to the couch. Carol cried out with pleasure as Harlan took her in a wild, glorious meeting of minds and hearts, showing her with each adoring touch how he wanted her for his wife.

Harlan lay awake long after Carol had fallen asleep in his

arms. He had convinced her to wear his ring—would he be able to convince her to marry him? He knew that her doubts were legitimate, but how could they deny the love and passion they shared?

"Oh, Harlan, look at those dainty little fingers!" Carol said softly as she stuck her finger into Heather's hand. The baby's hand immediately tightened around her finger. "Boy, has she got a grip. Look at that." Carol raised her finger and Heather held on tightly.

"I didn't know little babies were so strong," Kim admitted.

"Or so cute," Brandon added. He took the baby and laid her in his lap. "And she doesn't even cry that much."

At that moment Heather let out a howl. "Sure, she doesn't." Harlan laughed. "Do you want to come to Granddaddy, ladybug?"

"It's about suppertime," Kim said. "You can hold her after I feed her."

Kim opened her blouse and covered herself discreetly with a towel. Heather immediately stopped crying and settled down to nurse.

"Kim, Brandon, Carol and I are planning to get married," Harlan said quietly.

Kim and Brandon looked startled for a minute before they smiled. "Gonna make an honest man of him, Carol?" Brandon teased.

"Look who's talking!" Carol shot back.

They all laughed. "Well, congratulations," Brandon said as he extended his hand to Harlan.

"I'm happy for you, Mom," Kimberly said.

Brandon turned to Carol. "Do you realize that you're going to be both my mother-in-law and my stepmother?" he asked.

"Get me a bigger broom to ride," Carol teased.

They exchanged bad stepmother jokes for a few minutes, then Harlan and Brandon left to buy a pack of cigarettes. Kim turned anxious eyes on her mother.

"I really love the idea of you and Harlan getting married, so don't take me wrong, but do you really think you can make it together, Mom? You and he are so different!"

Carol got out a cigarette and lit it. "I hope so, Kim," she said quietly. "I know we have differences, but we love each other very much in spite of them."

"You're not sure, are you, Mom?" Kim asked quietly.

"No," Carol admitted softly, "God forgive me, but I'm not."

CHAPTER TEN

Carol blotted her lipstick and backed away from the mirror, observing herself critically. The cream-color lace blouse and satin skirt were a far cry from her business clothing, and her artfully tousled hair was quite different from her usual sleek style. She looked feminine and festive, not the way she usually looked at the office, but since the Christmas party was being held at a local hotel and not in the offices, it was all right. Besides, Harlan hadn't seen her really dressed up since the wedding, and she wanted him to see her at her best.

Carol tucked her lipstick and house key into a small clutch bag and turned out the bedroom light. She had heard Harlan let himself in a few minutes ago and found him reading a magazine in the family room. "Sorry you had to wait," she said as he stood up. "My, don't you look nice tonight."

Harlan grinned crookedly. "Do you think I'll pass muster with your fellow stockbrokers?"

"I think you'll outshine most of them," Carol said appreciatively as she took in Harlan's beautifully cut suit, the one she had helped him pick out last week when he insisted that nothing he had looked nice enough to wear to her company's party. "You look wonderful."

"So do you," Harlan said, kissing her temple lightly. "Are you ready to go?"

"Yes, finally," Carol teased as they left the house.

"Do your colleagues know you're getting married?" Harlan asked when they were in the car.

"I'm introducing you as my fiancé," Carol said quietly as she wondered how Harlan would fit in with the people he would encounter that night. Her colleagues tended to be sophisticated people on the way up in life, and in spite of his clothing and his good looks, it wouldn't take them long to figure out that Harlan wasn't in their league, nor did he want to be. She only hoped he wouldn't feel too out of place, because as her husband he would be expected to attend various functions like this with her from time to time.

Harlan too was wondering how he was going to fit in that night. Although he knew he looked all right, he wondered what on earth he and her colleagues were going to find to talk about. Did Carol's fellow stockbrokers share her deep need to succeed? What kind of people were they? Harlan only hoped that the evening wasn't going to be disappointing for either one of them.

Harlan parked the car in the hotel parking lot and Carol took his arm as they entered the building. They made a good-looking couple and they both knew it as they strode across the lobby.

"The party room's on the top floor," Carol said as they stepped into the elevator.

The event was in full swing as they entered the room, but a number of heads turned anyway. Bennie Johnson had spread the word that Carol Venson was getting married again, and Carol's fellow stockbrokers were curious as to the kind of man she would choose.

Harold Rhodes made a beeline for them and extended his hand. "Carol, I'm so glad you could come," he said.

"Thank you. Harold, I'd like you to meet my fiancé, Harlan Stone. Harlan, this is Harold Rhodes."

The men shook hands. "Your name sounds familiar," Harold said.

"My son's married to Carol's daughter," Harlan said.

"Oh, certainly," Harold said. "Congratulations to you both, and do enjoy the party."

"Thank you, I'm sure we will," Harlan said.

"Come on, I'll introduce you around," Carol said.

They spent the next half hour making their way around the room. Carol made a point to introduce him to every stockbroker in the office, and was delighted with the way Harlan charmed everyone. Stone's Tree Service was known all over Houston, and Carol was amazed at the ease with which her fellow stockbrokers accepted Harlan. Of course, he looked the part tonight, and because of the demands of his business, he knew quite a bit about taxes and investments and could talk intelligently about topics of mutual interest. But Carol couldn't help wondering cynically if Harlan would have received the same kind of respect if he had knocked on one of their front doors, dressed in his work clothes, to trim their trees.

Harlan smiled and shook hands and chatted with Carol's fellow stockbrokers, wondering as he did so how she could work with these barracudas every day and not go crazy. It wasn't that they were snobs; far from it. When Carol had introduced him as the owner of his own business, Harlan could see their eyes light up, and he was certain that he would be inundated next week with a deluge of telephone calls about investing his money with them, even though he was engaged to one of their colleagues. It bothered him that these people were so success-oriented that they would undercut a colleague. They couldn't even relax and enjoy a party like he could—he certainly had no intention of calling them next week and hustling their business! Although Harlan was enjoying the party and making a good impression on Carol's colleagues, he knew that he didn't fit in with this high-pressured, achievement-oriented group of people.

But, more important, he could see that Carol didn't, either. Underneath the tough businesswoman facade she presented to the world, Carol was a gentle person. She was sensitive and took things to heart, which was why her stomach couldn't take the kind of work she did. He didn't understand why Carol couldn't see that she was different from these people, but apparently she couldn't, and she wasn't going to appreciate it when he pointed it out to her.

They helped themselves to the generous buffet and sat down, balancing their plates on their laps. Harold Rhodes joined them. "Are you enjoying the party?" he asked.

"Lovely," Carol said, sampling a boiled shrimp.

"I've enjoyed meeting Carol's colleagues," Harlan said.

"I hope you plan to continue working after you're married," Harold said to Carol.

"Of course," Carol said, startled. "The days when married women went home are over, Harold."

"Just making sure," he said to both of them. "I don't want to lose one of my best stockbrokers." He turned to Carol. "I want to talk to you the week after Christmas," he said quietly.

"All right," Carol replied, hoping her expectation didn't show. There was a position opening for a vice-president, and she hoped against hope that Harold would offer it to her.

"What does he want to talk to you about?" Harlan asked as Harold walked off.

"I don't know," Carol hedged. She didn't want to say anything to Harlan until she had definitely been offered the job.

They stayed for another hour, and Harlan was quiet as he drove Carol home.

"Did you enjoy the party?" she asked as she hung her coat in the closet.

"Not really," Harlan said honestly.

"Why? Did anyone treat you badly?"

"No, nobody was a snob when they found out I'm not a professional," Harlan said dryly. "I think they could hardly wait to try and hustle my business next week."

"Well, I guess that's to be expected," Carol said as she sat down beside Harlan. "It's a wonder they didn't crack out their cards and hand you one."

Harlan grinned and pulled two business cards from his pocket. Carol read the names and laughed. "It figures."

"I can't understand how you manage to work around them day after day and not go crazy," Harlan observed. "They'd drive me around the bend."

"They're not such a bad bunch," Carol said defensively. "Remember, Harlan, I'm one of them."

"No, you aren't," Harlan said. "You don't fit in with that crowd at all."

"Thanks a lot," she said stiffly.

"Carol, I meant that as a compliment," Harlan said impatiently. "You're not like them, and if you'd take an honest look at yourself, you'd see that."

"But I *am* like them," Carol argued. "I'm sorry if that bothers you. But I do the same job they do—I do a better job than most of them, and I resent it that you're trying to make me feel like I don't belong in that circle."

"Well, you don't," Harlan said firmly. "They're a bunch of hard-driving hustlers. They can roll with the punches and go on. You're not like that. You're a sensitive, caring woman who's stomach hurts all the time because you're in a profession that's wrong for you."

"I can't believe this," Carol said. She rose from the couch and went over to stare out the window. "You know what I think, Harlan? I think you're jealous."

"What?" Harlan demanded.

"I think that, deep down, you're jealous of me. You're jealous of my education, my career, and my success. It came home to you tonight when you saw me with the people I work with. Oh, you say you don't want it for yourself, but deep down, you really do."

"That's ridiculous," Harlan said calmly. "Why should I be jealous of you for having something that's making you miserable? That makes you physically ill? Yes, I resent your career, Carol, because I'm tired of seeing the woman I love tired and tense and sick from it. But believe me, I'm not jealous of you. If that's what success costs, I'll stay a failure."

"All right, I'll admit that it's rough," Carol conceded. "But the money and success are worth it to me."

"Are you really that greedy?" Harlan asked incredulously. "You already make more money than you can enjoy."

"I wouldn't call it greedy, Harlan," Carol said angrily. "It's not the money, you know that. It's the success. Don't you understand? I screwed up when I was young. I failed, Harlan. I had to get married, then that marriage didn't work and I didn't even get my degree until I was twenty-nine. I'm making up for that now."

"You're being ridiculous," Harlan said hotly. "I'm sorry, but I don't see where conceiving Kim and spending a few years raising her is such failure. And I sure can't see where divorcing a fool like Jack can be construed as failing. You succeeded as a person those years, Carol. You're still succeeding as a person."

"Wonderful."

"No, damn it, I mean it," he snapped. "You've got this notion that being a stockbroker is the same as being a successful human being, and it's not. You're already a successful human being—you've raised a lovely daughter, you're a good mother-in-law, and you're a wonderful grandmother. What more do you want?"

"But that's not success," she said defensively. "Success is—"

"Success is money and power," Harlan said bitterly. "And you're going to sacrifice everything to earn it, aren't you? Even your own health. Damn it, Carol, when are you going to see the light?"

Carol swallowed as Harlan turned and left. She wanted to go after him, but she stood rooted to the floor. What good would it do to go after him that night? They would only argue more.

Carol showered and washed the stale cigarette smoke out of her hair. She lay staring up at the ceiling, too upset to even cry. Harlan simply couldn't—or wouldn't—understand why her career was so important to her. Her doubts about their future loomed before her once again. She knew Harlan planned to give her a ring for Christmas, and she wasn't sure whether she should accept it from him, with this major disagreement still between them.

Carol sighed as the telephone rang. It was only two days until Christmas, and everyone was calling her, seeing if she could sell something so they would have a little extra money for Christmas gifts. Her stomach had been acting up since early that morning, and if she hadn't been so determined not to let the pain from her ulcer and her fight with Harlan get her down, she would have thrown in the towel and gone home. But she was determined to prove to both herself and Harlan that she wasn't too weak or too sensitive to succeed in her job. I'm not in the wrong profession, she thought again. He's just resentful of my success, that's all.

Carol answered the telephone and made a face when her caller identified himself. "Yes, Mr. Walsh, I'm aware that just last week you lost a considerable sum of money," Carol said, clutching the edge of the desk. "Sometimes that happens, no matter how hard I try to prevent it."

"That's ridiculous!" Joe Walsh snapped. "I should be making money, not losing it."

"Again, I apologize," Carol said. "But that's the nature of the stock market. Sometimes the best of us are caught unaware."

"It better not happen again, Mrs. Venson, or I'll be taking my business elsewhere," Mr. Walsh said angrily. He slammed down the receiver in her ear.

Carol hung up the telephone. "I wish you would," she said out loud.

She looked up and saw Ralph Macon standing in the doorway. "Got that money for me yet?" he asked eagerly. "Vera's going to be so excited! I'm supposed to pick up the coat this afternoon." Ralph had a CD coming due this month, and he had called her in the morning and asked her to cash it in so he could pay for his wife's sable.

"I'll do that right now," Carol said. "Have a seat."

Ralph perched on the edge of the chair as Carol got out her book and looked up the number of Ralph's CD.

Her stomach knotted when she realized her mistake. "Ralph, this CD doesn't mature for another month," she said quietly.

Ralph's eyes widened. "But when I called this morning, you said I could get the money today!"

Carol fought not to wince. "I made a mistake, Ralph," she explained. Oh, why had she relied on her memory instead of looking up the damned number? Because she was still distracted by her argument with Harlan, that was why. "You can't take the money out for another month without incurring a substantial penalty."

Ralph's face fell. "I was counting on that money to buy Christmas gifts for the family, not just Vera's coat," he said. "It's too late to get the money somewhere else. My bank's not open tomorrow."

"Maybe not," Carol said quickly. "Let's see—"

"No. I don't want to start screwing around with any of my other investments," Ralph said bitterly. He shrugged. "I guess we can have Christmas next month."

"Let me work on it before you give up. We have the rest of today and tomorrow."

"All right. Call me if you come up with the money."

Carol bit her lip as Ralph left her office. She would have felt better if he had yelled at her. She felt terrible about letting him down and inwardly railed at herself for not looking in the book before she had blithely assured him the CD would provide money for Christmas.

Carol pushed herself through the rest of her workday and cursed the heavy traffic that she ought to be used to by this time. After last night, she wasn't sure whether or not Harlan was going to come and help her put up her tree as they had planned, and she almost hoped that he wouldn't. Her stomach had hurt continuously the whole day, and her medication was proving ineffective.

Harlan's car was sitting in the driveway, and a huge Christmas tree was propped on the front porch.

"Harlan?" Carol called as she opened the door.

Harlan reached for her and enveloped her in a loving embrace. "I'm sorry," he said as he cradled her in his arms. "I didn't want to fight last night."

"I didn't, either," Carol said as she hugged him back.

"I brought hamburgers and we can put up the tree. Do you have to work tomorrow?" Harlan asked.

"Yes, for a little while at least," Carol said. "I managed to screw up this morning and I have a client with no money for Christmas. I have to finagle him some money for presents."

"How much?" Harlan asked.

"About sixty thousand," Carol said.

"Good lord, what's he buying?"

"A sable coat."

"My *house* didn't cost that much!" Harlan said unbelievingly.

"Neither did my first one," Carol admitted.

Carol forced down half of her hamburger as she thought about how to come up with money for Ralph Macon and struggled to keep the continuing pain in her stomach at bay. It was getting worse, but she didn't want Harlan to know. He would just become angry that she was letting her job bother her so much.

They put the dishes in the dishwasher and Harlan brought in the tree. Carol's stomach grew continually more painful as they strung up lights and hung ornaments. Harlan glanced several times at her pinched, white face. "What's wrong?" he finally asked.

"It's my stomach. It's killing me."

"Why didn't you say something?" Harlan demanded. "Sit down and I'll bring you a pill."

"Don't bother, they aren't doing any good," Carol admitted as she collapsed on the couch.

Harlan touched her forehead and found it clammy. "Good grief, Carol, you should be in bed," he said. "Who's your doctor?"

"I don't need the doctor."

He stroked her hair gently. "Come on, let me call him."

Carol gave in and Harlan made the call from the kitchen.

"He's calling a stronger painkiller into the drugstore at the shopping center," Harlan said when he returned. "And he wants you to make an appointment to see him after Christmas."

"Thanks," Carol said weakly as she lay back on the couch.

Harlan knelt beside her. "Why didn't you tell me you were sick?"

"You would have fussed at me," Carol said softly. "I didn't want to be fussed at."

"I wouldn't fuss at you when you're sick," Harlan said soothingly as he kissed her forehead. "I'll be back in a little while."

Harlan pulled on his coat and stepped out into cold night air. His lips thinned in a grim line. No, he wouldn't scold her now, when she was sick, but when she felt better he would have plenty to say. He only hoped that, after this, she would have the sense to listen.

Harlan came back with the medicine twenty minutes later. "The druggist said this stuff would make you woozy, and he said you ought to take it and go to bed."

"But it's early," Carol protested as she rolled off the couch.

"Carol, you need the rest," Harlan said. "I'll stay tonight and make sure you're all right."

"You don't have to, but thanks," she said quietly.

She took a dose of the medicine and showered while Harlan put away the ornament boxes. He was sitting on the bed waiting for her when she came out of the bathroom. "I see what he meant about the medicine," she admitted as she pulled a nightgown over her head. "I feel a little dizzy already."

Harlan helped her pull on the gown. "Is it doing anything for the pain?" he asked anxiously.

"Wonders," Carol admitted. Harlan turned back the covers for her. "I don't need to go to bed yet, honestly."

He kissed her cheek. "Humor me."

"All right," Carol said. She got into bed and pulled the covers up. "I'm sorry I was a bother tonight."

"You weren't a bother," Harlan reassured her as he kissed her again. "I'll wait here until you've gone to sleep."

Carol snuggled down into the covers and a few minutes later her even breathing told Harlan the medicine had taken complete effect. He went to the kitchen and sighed as he mixed himself a drink. Carol was killing herself at the profession she had chosen, but she became furious at the thought of giving up her work and going into something less demanding. Why couldn't she understand that no profession and no amount of money was worth that? Was her sense of values actually that warped? Harlan thought of confronting her in the morning, but he decided that maybe he would have better luck waiting to talk with her after Christmas. She'd be wearing his ring then, and maybe that would give him a little more influence with her.

Carol lay back on the pillow and held her new diamond ring up to catch the morning sunlight that streamed through the window. "This has to be the most beautiful ring in the world," she said as she tilted the pear-shaped diamond back and forth, catching the light of the sun and reflecting it onto the far wall.

"No, you just think it is," Harlan teased as he kissed the ring and her finger. "It's not even all that big. You probably could have bought yourself a bigger one."

"Yes, but it wouldn't have been a gift of love," Carol said as she snuggled up to Harlan. "Besides, you can give me a sable like Vera Macon's someday."

Harlan pretended to give it some thought. "Maybe I can swing it for Valentine's," he said. "How did you manage to get the man that kind of money so quickly?"

"One of Ralph's stocks had risen in value but was starting to fall slightly, so he agreed to sell it on Christmas Eve," Carol said. "Divine powers that be, save me from any more of those kinds of mistakes!"

"How could you have made a mistake like that, anyway?" Harlan asked.

"I was still upset from arguing with you, and I just didn't

check the date. I'll sure never be that careless again!" Carol was looking at her diamond and missed the wince that crossed his face. "Do you think Heather enjoyed her first Christmas?" she asked.

"I don't think she noticed," Harlan replied. "Did the kids seem all right to you?" he added. "With each other, I mean."

"I thought so, but then I was so absorbed with Heather I wouldn't have noticed," Carol admitted. She rolled out of bed and groaned. "I don't want to go to work," she complained. "I want to stay in bed with you all day."

"Likewise," Harlan said as he got up.

They shared a shower and Harlan made breakfast while Carol finished dressing. She sat down across from Harlan and buttered a slice of toast. "Our breakfast habits have improved since you started spending so much time over here," she observed as she poured herself a cup of coffee.

"Should you be drinking that?" Harlan asked quietly. "Won't it bother your stomach?"

"My stomach's fine," Carol assured him. "Thanks to the medicine you got me the other night."

Harlan blew on his hot coffee. "Carol, I've been meaning to talk to you about that night," he said, ignoring the way her face tightened. "You were really sick, and it was your job that triggered the pain. Is there any way you can ease up some at work?"

"And have Harold the Peril all over me about not meeting my goals?" Carol asked dryly. "No, Harlan, there's no such thing as letting up in stockbroking. With a twenty-percent client attrition rate every year, I have to keep swimming forward just to stay in place."

"But you're increasing your client base, according to what Harold told me at the party," Harlan said. "That means you're taking on more work all the time."

"I can handle it," she replied tersely.

"No, you can't," Harlan said impatiently. "Your body was

trying to tell you something the other night. You're working too hard and subjecting yourself to too much stress."

"Maybe if you hadn't picked a fight the night before, I wouldn't have made that kind of mistake," Carol said hotly. "My stomach was hurting before Ralph Macon walked in expecting his money."

"Oh, no. You can't lay all the blame on me," Harlan said. "You had an ulcer long before I ever met you. You're letting your job ruin your life."

"Damn it, Harlan, I am not! What's this all about this morning? Do you think you're going to turn into a chauvinist like Jack now that I have your ring on my finger?"

"Don't you ever equate me and that idiot ex of yours in the same breath!" Harlan said angrily. "He was a chauvinist—I'm just worried about you."

"No, you're not," Carol said. "If you were worried about me, you wouldn't keep picking these fights over my career. I still think that deep down, you resent my income and my life-style."

"Oh, pardon me for thinking that after the other night you'd be willing to see reason. But no, if a painful ulcer attack can't knock some sense into you, I won't be able to, either. You're too damn obsessed with success to care what it's doing to you."

"That's not fair, Harlan."

"But it's true," he retorted. He tried to swallow the rest of his toast, but it stuck in his throat. "Suit yourself. I'll see you tonight."

Harlan threw on his jacket and left. Carol rubbed her aching temples and debated whether or not to take a couple of buffered aspirin. "What a way to begin an engagement," she said dryly as more doubts about marrying Harlan flooded her thoughts. Maybe they would have been better off simply remaining lovers.

Licking her lips as she walked toward Harold Rhodes's office, Carol tried not to appear too anxious. She had gotten a message that Harold wanted to see her as soon as the stock exchange closed, and if he wanted to talk about that vice-presidency, she was going to leave his office a very happy woman. She knocked and Harold called out for her to come in.

"Have a seat, Carol. I'll be right with you," he said as he turned back to the inevitable telephone conversation.

Carol tried not to fidget as he finished his call. "Gets old, but it's necessary," he said after he hung up. "Did you have a nice Christmas?"

"Yes, lovely," Carol said.

"That's wonderful. I'm sure you and your fiancé are looking forward to many more together."

"That we are." Cut out the garbage, Harold, and get on with it, she thought.

"The reason I called you in this afternoon is to discuss the possibility of your taking the vice-presidential position when Arnie Maxim retires," Harold said. "Are you interested?"

Was he kidding? "Yes, of course," Carol replied.

"I think you'd be excellent," Harold said. "You perform well under pressure and aggressively seek out new business. And that's what we want. Of course, you'll also be making a better salary."

Harold spent a few minutes outlining the additional responsibilities the job would entail. It sounded like a lot of work, but landing a vice-presidency was something Carol had dreamed of for years.

"It sounds great, Harold," she said when he was finished.

"Don't accept until you talk it over with Harlan," Harold said. "Be sure he has no objections to the extra time and effort you'll have to put into this position."

"He'll have no objections," Carol stated. If he did, he better keep quiet about it, she added silently.

"You can give me your answer tomorrow," Harold said.

Carol drove home in a haze of excitement. She had been offered a vice-presidency! She had really made it, she had to have made it to have been offered that kind of promotion. She called Kim with the news, but decided to wait and tell Harlan in person. She worried for a moment about his reaction, but decided that he wouldn't be anything but happy for her when he had gotten used to the idea.

Carol had a festive table set in the dining room when Harlan let himself in. "Hello, we're celebrating tonight!" she called out from the kitchen.

Harlan stuck his head around the corner, not sure he had heard correctly. They had parted angry that morning and he had been half-afraid of his welcome. "What did you say?"

"We're celebrating," she repeated as she put the Cornish hens onto a platter.

"What are we celebrating?" he asked as he put his arms around Carol and kissed her soundly. "Our engagement?"

"Not exactly. We celebrated that last night." Carol poured green beans into a serving bowl. "I'll tell you about it after we eat."

Harlan tried to get Carol to share her secret, but she insisted that it wait until after dinner. She took the dirty plates into the kitchen and brought out pieces of leftover Christmas cake. "Sorry, it was the best I could do on short notice."

"Now may I ask what we're celebrating?" Harlan asked.

Carol extended her hand. "Meet the newest vice-president of Purcell-Smith," she said softly, her eyes sparkling with excitement.

Harlan looked down at her hand but made no move to shake it. "When did this happen?" he asked dully.

"It hasn't happened yet. Harold said to talk it over with you tonight, even though I told him that wasn't necessary," Carol said excitedly. "I'm going to tell him yes in the morning." She looked down at her hand. "Aren't you happy for me?"

"No, I'm not," Harlan said evenly. "At least, I don't think I am. How much additional work is this going to mean for you?"

"Some, but Harlan, this is an opportunity of a lifetime!" Carol said. "Do you realize how few people get that far?"

"So what?" Harlan exploded as he rose out of his chair. "Carol, you must be crazy if you think I'm going to let you take that promotion!"

Carol's eyes narrowed ominously. "I don't remember giving you the right to 'let' me do anything," she said, her voice dangerously quiet. "This is my decision, Harlan."

"That's where you're wrong!" Harlan bit out. "You're going to marry me—that means that if you make a foolish move like this, I have to live with the results of that move the same as you do. What are you thinking of, taking on additional responsibility? You can't handle the responsibility you already have!"

"I resent that, Harlan," Carol said hotly. "I handle my responsibilities just fine, or I wouldn't have been offered a promotion."

"Sure, you handle them so well I have to go out and get you stronger medicine for your abused stomach," Harlan jeered. "I'm sorry, but I've had it. I've taken as much of this success-at-any-price nonsense that I can. Either you refuse the promotion or I'm not going to marry you. It's as simple as that."

"Oh, really?" Carol asked angrily. "You think I'm going to fall for that old ultimatum bit? Forget it, Harlan. I'm calling your bluff."

"I'm not bluffing," he said, his voice low with anger. "I mean it. If you take that promotion, I walk out that door and the wedding's off. You have no business taking on that kind of job, Carol. For that matter, if you had any sense at all, you'd get out of stockbroking completely."

"And what do you suggest I do with my time?" she taunted, "crochet booties for Heather?"

"No, but you could find a job that's less stressful," Harlan said hotly. "For that matter, you could run Stone's Tree Service for me."

Carol looked at him, stunned. "And could you pay me a six-figure income to do it?"

"Of course not, but I—"

"Shut up, Harlan," Carol said. She jerked off her ring and threw it across the room, hitting Harlan in the chest with it. "Keep your damned ring. I don't want to run your tree-trimming business. I've been married once to a man who wanted to hold me back and make me his subordinate, and I'm sure as hell not marrying another one."

Harlan caught the ring as it bounced off his chest. His face was pale underneath his year-round tan. "Suit yourself," he said bitterly. "I've had it with you. You're welcome to destroy yourself for your career if that's what you want, but I'm not sticking around to watch you do it. It hurts too damn much."

He put the ring in his pocket and walked out the front door. Carol stood rooted to the spot for a minute before one harsh sob, then another, tore through her body. She sat down on the couch and let tears of hurt and anger flow as she cried for a long time. Harlan had proven no different from Jack. His ego couldn't take her success and his behavior had proven that he would have spent the rest of their lives together trying to hold her back, trying to keep her from being the kind of professional success she wanted to be. And she had come too far to let a man—even a man she loved with all her heart—do that to her.

CHAPTER ELEVEN

Carol entered the Purcell-Smith offices and went straight to Harold Rhodes's office. She knocked and hoped Harold wouldn't notice the deep circles under her eyes that she had tried to camouflage with makeup. She had only slept a few hours last night, and this morning it showed.

"Come in," Harold said. "Did you talk things over with Harlan last night?"

"Yes, and I definitely want the job," Carol said decisively.

"Wonderful. I'm glad he agreed with you. I'd like you to begin your new duties as of the second. Do you like Susan Velasquez or would you rather hire your own secretary?"

"Why don't I give her a try?" Carol said blandly, letting Harold come to his own conclusion regarding Harlan. She would wait a few weeks, then quietly mention to Bennie and a few of the others that she and Harlan had changed their minds about marrying.

Carol spent a lonely New Year's alone, and on the second of January began her duties as a vice-president of Purcell-Smith. She moved to Arnie's larger office, with a small outer office for her secretary, and immediately plunged into the demanding job. The additional workload, particularly the pressure to increase the client base of the company, was a shock to Carol, even though she had been expecting more work, and by the end of the second week she had admitted to herself that she didn't like this position nearly as much as she had liked simple stockbroking. Nevertheless, she wasn't about to ask to be removed from the job. It was one more feather in her cap of success.

If Carol's days were pressure-filled and hectic, her nights were long and lonely. She missed Harlan terribly, missed him with an aching pain that never subsided. But she wasn't about to call him, not even to see how he was doing. She was still furious with him for his high-handed ultimatum. He had no right to issue that kind of demand and expect her to fall in—she had worked too hard to get where she was now to give it all up and run a tree-trimming business. If Harlan's ego couldn't take her success, she was better off without him.

But Carol had to admit that, be it Harlan's fault or hers, she had once again failed in a relationship with a man. Haunted by yet another failure in her life, Carol drove herself just that much harder at work, staying long after the others had gone or taking a bulging briefcase home with her and working until the wee hours of the morning. And predictably, her stomach began to bother her again. The doctor agreed to fill her order for the stronger painkiller once, and Carol ignored his nurse's advice that she make an appointment to see him very soon.

The only bright spots in Carol's life were Kim and Heather. Carol made it a point to drop in at least once a week on her way home to see the baby, and Kim frequently brought Heather over to Carol's on Saturday afternoon. Carol had finished cleaning her house and was wading through yet more paperwork when the doorbell rang one Saturday afternoon late in January.

"Kim! Oh, I was afraid you'd decided not to bring her out in the cold," Carol said as Kim carried in the big car carrier where Heather lay sleeping.

"I spent most of the afternoon in the library, and Brandon took off the minute I got home, so we got in the car and came over." Kim looked down at Heather, who was starting to wake up. "You're at Grandma's, punkin," she said softly. "Want to wake up and join the fun?"

Heather let out a few baby sounds. "Here, let me take her," Carol said as she lifted the baby and unwrapped the heavy blanket. "Ooh, Kim, she's getting bigger," Carol said as she sat down with the baby in her arms.

"Isn't she?" Kim said proudly. "She's let me sleep every night this week."

"Good for you, Heather," Carol said. Heather's eyes popped open and she gazed at Carol.

Carol talked baby talk and nonsense to Heather until the little girl started whimpering. "Here you go, Mommy," Carol said as Kim started unbuttoning her blouse. "Sorry, little one, Grandma can't help you there."

Kim sat back and cradled her nursing baby. "Will Brandon be gone long?" Carol asked. "If he is, I'd be glad to fix you supper here."

"I don't know," Kim said softly with a strange catch in her voice.

Carol looked up. "Is something wrong?"

"I'm afraid so," she admitted miserably. She lifted tear-filled eyes to Carol. "I don't think we're going to make it, Mom. We're trying, we really are, but it's just not working."

Carol groaned inwardly. Another divorce, another child without two full-time parents, and another young woman's life starting out with a failure. "Do you want to talk about it?" she asked quietly.

Kim shook her head quickly. "Thanks, Mom, but this is something Brandon and I have to try to work out on our own. It's time we quit running to you and Harlan with our problems. It looks like you two have enough of your own."

"You mean we weren't smart enough to make things work, either," Carol said dryly.

Kim blushed. "That wasn't what I meant."

Carol laughed without humor. "No, you're right. We didn't even make it as far as the ceremony. Ah, hell. I had hoped so much that this marriage of yours was going to make it. I've even learned to love Brandon."

Kim wiped a tear off her cheek. "Thanks, Mom, I love him too."

"Kim, if there's anything I can do to help you, please ask."

"I will. But please don't worry about us. We'll make it if it was meant to be."

But Carol did worry about Kim and Brandon. She hated the thought of the young couple divorcing and depriving Heather of a full-time father, and she hated the thought of Kim having to raise Heather alone. But mostly she hated the thought of her daughter beginning life with the same sense of failure that had plagued her for years—one that still plagued her, to a certain extent.

The work, the worrying, the missing Harlan—Carol's problems and the stress she was under began to take its toll. Her stomach ached night after night, keeping her awake long after she had gotten into bed. It hurt so badly at times that she couldn't eat, and she lost weight she didn't need to lose. Her stomach pills were no longer effective in easing the pain, and when the spasms got really bad at night she would have to resort to the more powerful medication. She knew she should make an appointment with the doctor, but she kept putting it off, telling herself that her stomach would get better when she had settled into her job.

"Susan, did you ever reach Ralph Macon? That stock's dropping by the hour! If I don't unload it soon, he's going to lose a bundle." Carol flipped through the Rolodex for the telephone number of another client who had the same stock.

"His office just says that he's out, and no one answers at his house," Susan said.

"Worth at least five million, and he won't get a pager," Carol murmured disgustedly.

"Is there a stop order on the stock?" Susan asked anxiously.

"No, the idiot won't even issue me one of those," Carol said. "Keep trying him."

Susan kept trying to reach Ralph while Carol telephoned her other clients who held the stock. She managed to reach most of them and get authorization to sell, but she still hadn't reached

Ralph by the time the exchange had closed, and he had already lost a hefty sum of money. Carol put her head in her hands for a minute, willing the sharp pain in her stomach to ease up.

Carol's intercom buzzed. "I finally reached Ralph's housekeeper," Susan said. "He's on vacation and won't be back until Monday."

Carol snapped a curse word that made Susan blush. "He's going to lose a fortune, the fool."

She hung up and almost immediately the phone rang. "Carol, did you ever get in touch with John Makarsky? He still owes a hundred thousand on that trade he made last month and my client's screaming," Harold snapped.

And I'm about to join him, Carol thought. "I'll get hold of John today," she promised.

As she had expected, John hedged and said he would have the money next week, and Carol had the thankless task of calling Harold with the news. Predictably, Harold was put out and made no secret of it. Carol's stomach twisted in a particularly agonizing spasm as she hung up the phone. Why had she ever thought she *wanted* this job?

The pain grew increasingly worse, and by the time the other stockbrokers started to drift out of the office, Carol had broken out in a cold sweat. She took a couple of pills, almost throwing them back up in the water fountain, but made it to the parking lot and collapsed into her car. Her head was swirling and she rolled down the window, hoping the cold air would clear her head. Thankfully, the pills started to take effect by the time she had reached the freeway, and she made it home safely.

Carol tried to eat dinner, but it came up almost immediately. She took some of the stronger medicine, but her stomach rejected it also. The pain was becoming more intense by the minute and by the middle of the evening Carol could no longer even sit up straight. She realized that this was no simple stomachache—she was sick and needed help. She called the doctor's answering service and he called her back just a few minutes later.

"Is your stomach acting up again this evening?" he asked jovially.

Dr. Harmon became increasingly less jovial as Carol described her symptoms. "I'm still here at the hospital. Meet me here as soon as you can."

"Where can I park?" Carol asked.

"Park, my foot. You get someone to bring you. And plan on staying overnight."

"But I can't!" Carol protested to a dial tone. Wincing, she called Kim's number and prayed that Brandon would be home.

Brandon himself answered. "Brandon, this is Carol," she said softly. "I have to go to the hospital, and I'm too sick to drive myself. Can you take me?"

"Of course," Brandon said instantly. "We'll be right there."

"Oh, don't drag Heather out in the cold," Carol protested weakly.

Carol was trying to pack a bag when Brandon arrived. With touching masculine ineptness, he helped her pack and carried her to his truck, gently placing her in the passenger seat. "I thought this might be more comfortable tonight than the sports car," he explained as he got in beside her.

"Thanks," Carol said. Her eyes brimmed with tears as she glanced over at Brandon. He had so many of the same qualities that she loved in Harlan! The thought of Brandon and Kim divorcing nearly broke her heart.

Dr. Harmon met her in the emergency room. He examined Carol carefully and ordered X-rays. Carol managed on the second try to keep down enough of the wretched barium to make an X-ray, and they finally wheeled her to a room where a nurse helped her into her gown. The IV they started dripping into her vein must have had something powerful in it, because Carol shut her eyes and knew no more until morning.

"Mrs. Venson? Are you awake?"

Carol turned her head on the pillow and stared at the cheerful aide. "I am now," she said dryly.

"Here's your breakfast," the girl said, setting the tray on the stand. "Would you like to sit up?"

Carol nodded and the girl raised the head of the bed. "Push this little button if you need anything else."

Carol said she would and took the lid off the meal. She grimaced when she saw the Cream of Wheat, but figured she couldn't be too sick if Dr. Harmon had ordered it for her. Miraculously, her stomach didn't hurt her at all that morning, although she expected that it would once she got out of there and back to the office. She called Harold and told him she was ill, neglecting to mention that she was in the hospital. She didn't want him to know how sick she had been last night.

Carol wasn't very hungry, but she made a valiant effort to eat. She showered and was about to get back into bed when a young nurse came and took her to be weighed and have her blood pressure measured. She had just returned from that when Dr. Harmon poked his head around the corner.

"Having a nice rest?" he asked, smiling at her.

"Not this morning," Carol said. "But yes, I slept well last night. That was some nightcap you shot into me."

"Well, I figured you could use the rest." Dr. Harmon got out Carol's chart and sat down in a chair beside the bed. "Carol, you and I need to have a serious talk about the effect stress is having on your body."

"I'm listening," she said quietly.

"I hate telling you this, but you've got to get out from under the stress you live with," Dr. Harmon said. "You need to find another type of job. Your body simply can't take any more abuse. Not only is your stomach worse, but you've lost ten pounds since your last office visit and your blood pressure's sky-high."

"But what will I do?" Carol protested. "I have to work."

"But you don't have to work as a stockbroker," he said firmly. "Look, I'm no job counselor, but I am your physician, and I'm telling you that you don't have more than two or three years to live if you don't slow down. You'll have a heart attack or a stroke, or that ulcer will perforate. I mean it, Carol. You keep this up and you won't see forty."

Carol swallowed. "You really mean that, don't you?"

"I sure do," Dr. Harmon said. "It's your choice, Carol. Make a change or you'll have to face the consequences."

The doctor gave her another prescription for her stomach and said he would arrange for her release. Carol stared into space for a few minutes, letting what Dr. Harmon told her sink in. Forty. If she didn't slow down, she wouldn't see forty. She wouldn't see Kim get her degree and start a career, and she wouldn't get to watch Heather grow up.

The nurse brought her release papers, and Carol telephoned the tree service and asked to have Brandon paged. He called a few minutes later and said he would come get her immediately, if she didn't mind him coming in his work clothes.

She was dressed and waiting when Brandon came to her room. "Are you all right?" he asked anxiously. "You're still awfully pale."

"No, I'm okay," she replied.

Brandon carried her suitcase out to the truck. "What did the doctor say?" he asked as they left the hospital parking lot.

"Stress," Carol said simply. "Too much stress."

"Your job?" Brandon asked.

"It looks like I have to give it up. But there were other things too, like breaking off with your father."

"Were some of those other things Kim and me?" Brandon asked tightly. "Has Kim talked to you?"

"She didn't confide, if that's what you mean. She did say that you were having some problems. Naturally I'm worried, Brandon. I don't want her to divorce you."

Brandon smiled faintly. "Thanks."

They drove to Carol's home in silence and Brandon carried in her suitcase. Carol sat down in the kitchen while he made them both lunch, and she couldn't help but notice that he looked as miserable as Kim had the other day.

"Would you like to talk to me about it?" she asked as Brandon put a grilled cheese sandwich in front of her.

"You'll just take her side."

"Like I did on Thanksgiving?" She paused. "Come on, Brandon, I love you like a son. Talk to me, please, or I'm going to start worrying again."

"Kim's been offered a scholarship to Rice for next fall," Brandon said. "And she's mad because I don't want her to take it."

"Why not?" Carol asked. "Rice is a fine school."

"I know, but we don't have that kind of money," he said. "Even with a scholarship, it's going to cost a lot more than U of H."

"Brandon, I know you don't want to accept money from me, but I can afford any additional tuition easily," Carol said. "I can pay what Rice doesn't. It's my obligation as her mother."

"Still, that campus is way across town," Brandon complained. "She'll have to drive that every day, and go back sometimes at night too. She might get hurt or something!"

"It's not really all that far," Carol said mildly. "I understand that the campus is well lighted at night, and if you're all that worried you could always take her at night and pick her up later."

"Do you really think she'll want her tree-trimming husband to be seen on that campus with her?" Brandon asked bitterly.

Carol looked up and was astonished to see tears in his eyes. "Oh, Brandon, she won't feel that way!"

"How do I know that?" he asked miserably. "I'm so scared, Carol! Kim's so set on getting out in the world and being a success. And if she does, she'll outgrow me and I'll lose her and Heather. She'll divorce me and marry someone who's like she is."

"Why are you so sure of that?" Carol asked quietly.

"It happened to you and Dad, didn't it? He really loved you, but he wasn't a professional like you are and it didn't work," Brandon said.

"Is that what your father said?"

"No, he wouldn't say a word," Brandon said quickly. "He told me to mind my own business."

"You came to the wrong conclusion about Harlan and me, Brandon. And you're about to make the same mistake your father did, which is why I called everything off."

"What?"

"Your father never did like my career," Carol said. "He kept trying to undermine my confidence by telling me that I shouldn't be a stockbroker, that the job was all wrong for me. Finally, I was offered a vice-presidency at work and he said that he wouldn't marry me if I accepted the promotion."

Brandon winced. "And you told him where he could put it."

"I did," Carol admitted. "I didn't leave him because his job wasn't good enough for me. His job never entered into it. I left him because he tried to hold me back. He wouldn't support me in my chosen career. He's a good man, but in that he treated me no better than Jack did. I just won't put up with that. And neither will Kim, I'm afraid."

"But what if she decides I'm not fancy enough for her?" Brandon asked anxiously.

"Brandon, I can't guarantee you that Kim won't ever change her mind and decide that you're not good enough for her. But I can guarantee that you'll lose her if you try to hold her back and keep her from being the success she feels driven to be. Oh, she might give in this time, but sooner or later she's going to decide she's had enough and leave. Then again, she might leave you this time. She's pretty determined about her education these days."

"So you think I ought to shut up and take my chances?" Brandon asked.

"Brandon, I don't think you're taking all that big a chance. She loves you and she loves the child she conceived with you. And I promise you that you have all the love and support I can give you."

Brandon leaned over and kissed Carol's cheek. "You're the best mother-in-law a man ever had," he said softly. "Thanks."

"Thanks, yourself," Carol said.

Brandon cleaned up the kitchen and left Carol alone. She sat down in the family room and looked around at her beautiful home. If she took Dr. Harmon's advice and got out of stock-broking, she would probably have to give it up.

Carol smiled grimly. Why was she trying to kid herself? There was no way she could continue as a stockbroker, not if it meant killing herself. Her life meant more to her than her profession.

Tears filmed Carol's eyes as she looked around the house. Oh, she might be able to keep it, if she continued to have an income from the stock she already owned. But it wasn't the house, or the car, or the luxurious life-style, not really. It was the sweet taste of success that she hated giving up. It was the pride in succeeding in a demanding, difficult profession that she hated losing so much. But Carol had been in the profession long enough to know that there was no way she could ease up. The job was stressful by nature, and if she was going to remove the stress from her life, she was going to have to give up the profession completely.

A deep depression settled over Carol, and she spent most of the afternoon sitting in the rocking chair. She finally noticed that it was starting to get dark and was about to go fix herself something to eat when the doorbell rang. She started not to answer it, but it rang a second time, and a third.

Listlessly, Carol pushed herself from the rocker and peered out the peephole. Harlan stood on the other side of the door, glowering. What now? she thought disgustedly. She threw open the door, poised for battle.

"Do you *really* think I was just trying to hold you back?" Harlan demanded incredulously.

Carol eyed him warily. "You're not here to raise hell about me telling Brandon to let Kim go to Rice?" she asked.

"No. You probably saved that marriage," Harlan admitted. "Do you really think I was trying to hold you back?"

"Well, weren't you?" Carol asked defiantly.

"No, I was not," Harlan said. He took her by the shoulders and moved her aside so he could enter the house. "We're going to talk about this."

Considering that he was already in the house, there wasn't much Carol could do but follow him into the family room. "Sit down," he snapped, pointing at the sofa.

Carol sat down and stared up at the man pacing her floor. "I couldn't believe what Brandon said you told him," he said angrily. "I can't believe that you honestly think I just didn't want you to have a successful career. What kind of selfish bastard do you think I am?"

"All you ever did was gripe about my job," Carol said bitterly. "What was I supposed to think?"

"You were supposed to think that I cared about you!" Harlan yelled across the room at her. "You were supposed to think that you meant more to me than the things your money could buy!"

"I thought you resented my success," Carol said.

"Good grief, Carol! I don't care if you're the richest, most successful woman in Texas, as long as you don't kill yourself doing it!"

Carol ducked her head and bit her lip, trying not to cry. "You should have been a doctor," she said as the first sob escaped her. "He—he said the same thing to me this morning."

Carol buried her head in her hands and gave way to the bitter disappointment that she had felt all afternoon. Sobs shook her as she cried for all the years and hard work she had to give up. She was so lost in her misery that she was barely aware of it when Harlan sat down beside her and cradled her head on his shoulder. "Shh, Carol, I didn't mean to make you cry," he said as he stroked her soft hair. "I'm sorry."

She raised tear-filled eyes. "I've failed all around, haven't I? I have to give up stockbroking, Dr. Harmon told me so this morning, or it's going to kill me. I failed at it, Harlan. Eight long years of effort and I have to walk away from it! And I managed to lose you at the same time. I've failed at my job and I've failed with the man I love, so I guess that makes everything, doesn't it?"

Harlan looked around at Carol's beautiful home. "I'd hardly call you a failure, Carol. You've been very successful at what you do, in spite of the fact that a high-pressure job like stockbroking's not really the right thing for you. Why don't you think about how much more successful you'd be if you went into something that was right for you?"

Carol sniffed and looked at Harlan doubtfully.

"And as far as we're concerned," he continued, "I haven't stopped loving you. Once we get to the bottom of this mess, I'd still like to marry you, if you haven't changed your mind about me."

Carol accepted the handkerchief Harlan held out to her. "I don't know, Harlan," she said slowly. She blew her nose and stood up to pace the floor as he had done earlier. "Having to give up stockbroking's a blow, I'll be the first to admit, but I'll find something else. And whatever it is, Harlan, I'm going to be a success at it. I'm just made that way."

Carol stopped and put down the handkerchief. "That's what has me worried. You were angry at me for working so hard as a stockbroker. Are you going to fuss just as much when I'm working hard at my new career? I love you and I miss you terribly, but I have to have a career of some kind too. I can't just sit at home and be Carol Stone. And it's important to me to succeed in that career, Harlan, whatever it is. Being successful at whatever I do is terribly important to me. Can you understand that?"

"Come here," Harlan said as he patted the sofa. When Carol sat down, he took a piece of paper from his pocket with a list of names on it. "When Brandon told me this afternoon that you were going to have to give up your job, I made a few calls to some people I've worked for in the last few months."

Harlan pointed to the first name on the list. "This man's the vice-president of Challenger Savings," he said. "He's got two vacancies at the bank—one in the loan department and one as a trust officer. He desperately needs someone with investment experience in the trust department. I told him that I didn't know whether you were qualified for the job or not, but he's very interested in talking with you."

Harlan pointed to the second name. "Remember that crotchety old widow in River Oaks I was laughing about last summer? She's setting up a charitable foundation and needs an administrator who knows about investments. She said she'd give her eye teeth to have a former stockbroker in that position."

"I've heard of him," Carol said, pointing to a third name on the list. "He's one of the best stockbrokers at Merrill-Lynch."

"He's recovering from a heart attack," Harlan said dryly. Carol winced. "His doctor told him the same thing yours told you, only he didn't get told in time. Anyway, he wanted to know if you'd be interested in going into partnership with him. He's planning to start a financial planning service, where for a fee he and a client would sit down and make an overall financial plan. You did a lot of that as a stockbroker, didn't you?"

"Yes, and I always enjoyed it," Carol murmured.

"Hal said he could have the creativity without the pressure that way," Harlan commented. "And the last name here is one of the economics professors at U of H. He doesn't have a job to offer you, but he did suggest that you consider becoming a systems analyst. The only drawback to that is that you'd have to go back for your MBA."

Harlan hesitated a minute. "I know you rejected it before, but I still like the idea of you running Stone's Tree Service for me, if you wanted to. With you at the helm, we could expand it some without it killing either one of us, and we'd have a really nice legacy to hand down to the kids someday."

"I'll give it every consideration," Carol promised. She was quiet for a minute. "How many phone calls did this really take?" she asked finally. "You couldn't have gotten this much information from four lucky calls."

Harlan thought a minute. "Between twenty and twenty-five," he said.

"You spent the whole afternoon on the telephone looking for a job for me?" Carol asked incredulously.

"Yes, I did. And if none of these work out, I'll make more until something comes up that you think is right for you," Harlan said. "Admittedly, none of them is going to pay six figures at first, but you and Hal could probably be making close to your commissions as stockbrokers in a year or two, at least that's what he thinks. And securities analysts don't starve."

"And you'll support me in these," Carol said slowly.

"Yes, I will," Harlan said. "None of the possibilities have anywhere near the pressure that stockbroking does. I'll support you in anything you do, Carol, as long as you don't put your health in jeopardy. You're a bright, hard-working, ambitious person, but you just don't have the kind of personality that can take pressure. And there's no shame in that."

"But what if the job demands long hours?" Carol asked.

"Working long hours isn't necessarily stressful, is it? Carol, I mean it. As long as you aren't under stress, you're welcome to work long hours and rise to the top and make scads of money I can help you spend." He stopped and thought a minute. "But does it bother you that I don't care as much about being a success as you do? You've just had a major setback and you're already raring to go out there and make it big in a second profession. Can you live with the fact that I'm not going to get out there and do the same?"

Carol faced Harlan. "In all the time we were going together, did I once tell you that I thought you ought to expand, or grow, or change your business in any way?" she asked quietly.

Harlan thought a minute. "Never."

"And I never will," Carol assured him. "Stone's Tree Service is your business, and if you feel that it's as much as you want, that's fine with me. Of course I can live with the fact that you don't consider success all that important, as long as you'll try to understand that success in some form is very important to me."

Harlan captured her face between his palms. "Of course I can," he said as he bent his head to kiss her lips. "Oh, love, I've missed you so much!" he said as they melted together in a tender, passionate embrace.

Carol opened herself joyously to Harlan's kisses. They stayed there for a long time, wrapped in one another's arms as they kissed away the pain and bitterness of the last weeks. In spite of the disappointment of the day, Carol was where she was supposed to be, back in Harlan's arms, with his love and his strength supporting her again.

"Harlan, why did I ever let you walk out that door?" she murmured when their lips finally parted.

"I shouldn't have issued you that ultimatum," he said. "I knew that the moment I left here. I should have tried to work something out. I left you no choice."

"I didn't like the job," Carol admitted. "It was miserable, in fact."

"Hey, let's put that behind us, all right? Let's think of happier things." He took her ring from his shirt pocket. "I was hoping you'd put this back on," he said quietly.

Carol nodded, her throat thick with emotion. Harlan put the ring on her finger and kissed it back into place. They looked into one another's eyes for a moment, each seeing love and need and tenderness. Then Harlan opened his arms, and Carol flew into them. "I need you," she said. "Could we make love, please?"

Harlan shook his head. "Carol," he protested, "you just got out of the hospital!"

"I'll be careful," Carol promised. "Oh, Harlan, I need you so badly! I don't care if it's the wrong time of day, or that I've been sick. I need your loving."

He nodded slowly. "But we're going to be very careful," he warned her. He touched her midriff gently. "Is it sore?"

"A little," she admitted.

He took her hand and led her down the hall to her bedroom, then snapped on the light and sat down in the chair. "I need a shower," he said as he started pulling off his boots. "I came straight from work."

"I haven't even noticed," Carol admitted. "Mind if I join you?"

They stripped, and Harlan gasped when he saw Carol's naked body. "How much weight have you lost?" he demanded.

Carol looked down and grimaced. "It wasn't intentional."

Harlan grasped her by the shoulders and turned her to face him. "You'll never do this to yourself again," he said almost fiercely, his eyes sparkling with tears. "Carol, I've lost one woman I loved, I couldn't bear to lose another."

Carol swallowed. "I promise, Harlan," she said, her own voice thick. "I won't ever do this again, I promise."

Harlan wiped the tears out of his eyes. "That's why I left, you know. I couldn't stand what you were doing to yourself."

"Would you like me better if I got fat?" Carol teased.

"I wouldn't mind plump and sassy," Harlan admitted. "Come on."

Harlan washed Carol's too-thin body gently, and she let herself touch and caress the strong, sensitive man she had thought she would never be with again. They dried themselves and Harlan turned back the bed covers.

"I love you," he said as he lay down beside her on the bed. "Tell me if I hurt you."

"You won't hurt me," Carol assured him. "Love me, Harlan, I need that so much."

Harlan turned Carol over so that they were laying together spoon-fashion. His lips nibbled her nape as his hands cradled her breasts, rubbing each of her nipples with the tips of his thumbs.

"Harlan, I can't touch you from here," Carol complained as her breasts hardened into twin peaks of pleasure.

"That's the point," Harlan said, his breath moist on her skin. "I'm so ready to make love to you that it's all I can do not to roll you over and take you right now. It's been so long since we made love." His lips traveled down her back, tickling her spine and sending shivers through her body. He reached her waist and continued the trek downward.

"What are you doing?" Carol asked as his tongue swirled around the top of her bottom.

"There used to be a dimple here," Harlan complained. "I want my dimple back."

"All right, I'll eat like a horse until I've gained it all back," Carol promised.

"I want both little dimples back," Harlan said as he kissed the place where the other one used to be. "And I want you nice and round down here again." He took the sting from his words with tender caresses, loving Carol until she was spinning. He nibbled the back of her thighs and calves, discovering sensuous places Carol hadn't even known she had.

"When are you going to let me touch you?" Carol protested finally, not that she was really complaining. Harlan's touch was pure honey to her senses.

"Right now," Harlan said as he pulled himself up to lie facing her. "I wish you could see yourself through my eyes. You'd stop worrying about being a success. In my eyes you are a success, because you make me so very happy."

"You make me happy too, Harlan," Carol said as she touched him eagerly. Her fingers remembered the way his strong chest felt, how his masculine nipples would grow hard when she touched him, how his waist was firm and flat. She touched his scar, loving his imperfection as much as she did his perfection. Her fingers found and stroked his hips and his hard masculine bottom. "You still have your dimples," she teased as Harlan grew weak from her touch.

Wanting to savor the joy and the passion of their relationship, they took their time to rediscover the love they thought they had lost. When at last they could stand it no longer, Harlan rolled over on his back and pulled Carol on top of him, careful to exert no pressure on her sore stomach. Slowly she eased down on him, completing their union with a small gasp of delight. She was still for a moment, as they savored being together once more. Then they started to move together, Carol setting the pace and Harlan quick to respond to her cues. They loved with the familiarity of longtime partners, yet it was a new beginning as well. For the first time, they were coming together with no conflicts between them, no reservations holding them back.

Desire swirled around them, enveloping them in a sensual haze that blurred the edges of their awareness, leaving them focused only on each other. They stared into one another's eyes as they reached the pinnacle of delight, their minds and hearts mating as surely as their bodies.

Harlan held Carol above him, still looking into her eyes. "That was incredible," he said.

"You made it that way." Slowly, reluctantly, she moved from Harlan and snuggled down beside him. "Which of the jobs sounds the best to you?" she asked.

Harlan shrugged. "They all have their merits. Why don't you go ahead and talk to each of the people but wait until after we're married to go back to work? That way you'll have time to put together a wedding and hopefully get some rest."

"And get fattened back up," Carol teased as he ran his hand down her back.

Harlan kissed her tenderly. "I wouldn't have said it, but yeah." He sat up and reached for his underwear. "Speaking of which, it's suppertime and I'm hungry. Why don't I make us supper in bed? Then we can practice for our honeymoon."

Carol laughed as Harlan went out to the kitchen. She snuggled back down into the covers, smiling to herself. She wasn't sure what path her professional life would take. She might like one of the ideas Harlan had brought her, or she might run Stone's Tree Service after all, or she might come up with an idea of her own. But she would do something, and she knew now that, whatever she did, she would do it with Harlan's loving support. That made it all worthwhile.